Copyright © 2018 Kay Shanee
All rights reserved.
ISBN-10: 1717184375
ISBN-13: 978-1717184375

DEDICATION

This book is dedicated to my husband. Thank you for always supporting me in all of my craziness. It doesn't matter if I succeed or fail, you are always there. I love you baby!

ABOUT THE AUTHOR

Kay Shanee is a forty something wife and mother, born and raised in the Midwest. During the day she is a high school teacher. In her free time, she enjoys spending time with her family and friends. Her favorite pastime is reading romance novels by authors that look like her. She enjoys it so much that she decided to become one of them.

CONTENTS

Chapter		
	Acknowledgments	i
1	My Homie's Girl	Pg 1
2	Things Aren't Always What They Seem	Pg 18
3	Love Doesn't Hurt	Pg 36
4	Best Friends	Pg 51
5	Trapped	Pg 69
6	Age Ain't Nothin' But a Number	Pg 88
7	Time Table	Pg 111

ACKNOWLEDGMENTS

There are so many people that I would like to thank. First and foremost, I'd like to thank God for giving me the ability to put these words together. He knew about my dirty mind before I did and gave me the courage to share it with you all.

I'd also like to thank my husband. He's been my backbone since our first year of college and I am forever grateful for his love and support. Let me give a shout out to my kids, even though they had no knowledge of this book until it was pretty much done.

My family and friends that read my stories and gave me honest feedback. Honestly, there are too many of you to name and I don't want to leave any of you out. Just know that I appreciate your support and I thank you from the bottom of my heart.

1 MY HOMIE'S GIRL

"Aye man, whatchu gettin' into now?" I asked my homeboy Zane as we left the pool hall."

"Shit, nothin' really. I got this shorty that's been blowing me up. I might slide through her crib and get my dick wet," he replied.

"Nigga, you just can't do right. You got the perfect woman that's been holdin' you down for a good minute, puttin' up with all yo shit, and you just keep fuckin' up!" I shook my head.

"You know how it is. Bitches just be throwin' the pussy at me and it would be rude of me to ignore them," Zane laughed.

Zane seems to think this is a joke. He's been with his girl, Sage, for a little over a year. If he had any sense, he would've locked her ass down months into the relationship. She's a rare breed these days. Beautiful, intelligent, supportive, bangin' ass body, not ratchet in any way but will get grimy if pushed. The perfect combination of everything one would want in a partner. If I had seen her first, she'd already be Mrs. Brees Gordon. Instead, I'm sitting on the sidelines, watching my boy Zane, play with her heart and emotions, doing her dirty behind her back.

Sage and I have gotten close over the last three months. Whenever Zane is out doing dirt, she's been confiding in me and leaning on me for support. I don't have the heart to tell her the truth about all of the dirt that Zane is out here doing in these streets, but I do allow her my shoulder to cry on. As much as I hate to leave her hanging, I'm gonna have to fall back on being there for her. I feel a deep connection with my best friend's girl and if Zane keeps fucking up, I can only see that connection getting deeper.

"You act like Sage holdin' out or some shit. You ain't hurtin' for pussy nigga!" I told Zane.

"I know, I just..., I don't know man. I know Sage is the one, I'm just not ready to be with only one woman. But when I'm ready, she is it for me," Zane confessed.

"Well, for your sake, let's hope you're ready soon and she sticks around until that time. I'm out. I'll hit you up tomorrow."

We put our fist together, said goodbye, and went our separate ways. Today is Friday and it's been a long week. I don't really have any plans this weekend, except to relax.

It took me about thirty minutes to get home and as I pulled into my garage, I heard my text notification. I looked at my phone and saw a text from Sage.

Sage: Is he with you?
Me: No
Sage: He told me he was gonna be with you after work.
Me: He was. We went to the pool hall but now I'm home.
Sage: He won't answer my texts or calls. I'm so sick of his shit.

See, this is how it starts. Sage texts me looking for Zane. Eventually she gets tired of texting then she calls. She ends up crying on the phone and asks to come to my house or for me to come to hers. I can't keep doing this.

Sage: Brees?
Me: I'm here

Seconds later, my phone is ringing, with Sage on the other line.

"I know you know where he is!" she screamed into the phone as soon as I answered.

"Look Sage, I'm not trying to be in the middle of ya'll shit. Zane is my boy but he's your man. If you don't like how your relationship is going, you know what you need to do. But you can't keep puttin' me in the middle," I explained.

"But you're the only person I can talk to about him. You're the only one that understands."

"Actually, I don't understand. I don't mind---" I started before Sage interrupted.

"Can you just come over, please? This is the last time I'll ask. I just need someone to talk to."

I let out a deep breath and ran my hand down my face. I just told myself that I need to pull back. The last time this happened, Sage and I almost let things go too far. I can't be so sure I'm gonna be able to control myself if there's a next time.

"I don't think that's a good idea Sage. You know what happened before," I warned her.

"Brees, please. I need you," Sage pleaded.

"I'm sorry Sage. Zane is my best friend and this shit ain't right. Keep trying to call or text him. I gotta go," I quickly hung up.

I sat in my car, in my garage for a few more minutes, collecting my thoughts. It kills me to be so cold towards Sage but it's the only way that I can fight the feelings I have for her.

I made my way into my house, went straight to my bedroom, undressed and got in the shower. I stood under the hot water for a long time, thinking about Sage. Her soft lips, full breasts, and the sweetness between her legs. *Shit! Now my dick is hard!*

I quickly washed up, trying to shake the images of Sage out of my head but it's impossible. She's all I've been able to think about for the past two weeks. The last time she called me over to talk, things got out of hand. I can't even lie and say that I regret it happened. I hate that nothing can ever become of us.

Turning the water off, I opened the shower door and was startled by who stood before me.

"Sage! How did you get in here?" I asked, grabbing my towel and wrapping it around my waist. It did nothing to cover up my erection.

"You gave me your garage code a while back, remember?" she answered, as she stood at the entrance to my bathroom.

"What are you doing here? I told you this ain't a good idea," I reminded her.

"I know. I called him again and he finally answered."

"Okay, so why are you here?" I repeated.

"He didn't answer on purpose. It had to be an accident because I know he didn't mean for me to hear him fucking some bitch!" she screamed, hysterically. "I listened to him," she paused, "for ten minutes, giving what's supposed to be reserved for only me, to someone else. I hate him Brees and I'm done. I can't do this anymore!"

I pulled her into my chest and wrapped my arms around her as she cried. She was mumbling something that I didn't understand because her face was in my chest.

"Why can't he be more like you?" she asked, looking up at me, with sadness and longing in her eyes.

I looked at her for a long moment and couldn't stand it anymore. Before I could even talk myself out of it, my mouth was on hers, and our tongues wrestled like it was the WWE.

My towel fell to the floor and I lifted Sage by her voluptuous ass. She wrapped her legs around my waist, I walked into my bedroom, and we fell onto my bed. Our lips never parted as we both frantically removed her clothing.

I lifted my body away from hers, ripping her shirt open, causing buttons to fly everywhere. The leggings she wore were somehow already at her knees and she didn't have on any panties. I yanked them the rest of the way down and threw them to the side.

For the first time since they touched, our lips separated. Sage lay there, in just her bra, looking up at me, breathing hard. If stopping this was an option, now would be the time to do it. But that wasn't about to happen. *Fuck it!*

I attacked her mouth again, then slowly moved to her neck, licking and sucking, surely leaving passion marks. I made my way down to her breasts, pushing her bra up over them to give me full access. I guess that wasn't good enough for Sage because she reached behind her back and unhooked it to take it off and threw it to the side.

Using the tip of my tongue, I circle around one of her chocolate nipples while massaging the other. Sage moaned and I swear my dick has never in life been this hard. It's almost painful!

I continued working my tongue down her body, taking my time and enjoying every second. When I made it to her center, it glistened, and I ran my two fingers between her lower lips, licked them, smiling up at her.

"You taste good baby!" I told her. She smiled back.

I kissed the inside of each of her thighs and her body shuddered. Being face-to-face with Sage's pussy is something that I've only dreamt about. I dove in, tongue first, attacking her clit.

"Aahh!" Sage screamed.

With my hands holding her thighs in place, just in case she's a runner, I kissed, licked, and sucked on her pussy, leaving nothing untouched. Just a few minutes later, she screamed my name so loud, I'm sure my neighbors heard her.

"Oh my God Brees! Aahh, shit baby. I'm 'bout to cum!" she yelled. I didn't ease up on that pussy at all. Her screams made me go harder.

"Brees, baby please, it's too much," she called out, as she tried to scoot away.

I gripped her thighs tighter and she had no chance of getting away. Pushing my tongue as deep inside of her pussy as I could, I twirled it around and she lost her mind.

"Fuck! I'm cumin' Brees. Shit! Oh my Ga---Oh my damn!" She released all over my face and I continued to lap up her juices.

I stood up, Sage barely had her eyes opened and her chest moved up and down. Mounting her, I gently pecked her forehead, as I hovered over her.

"You good?" I asked.

"I'm great," she responded, grabbing both sides of my face bringing my lips to hers.

We tongued each other down, as Sage spread her legs wide open, allowing my dick to press against her naked center.

I couldn't wait any longer so I grabbed my dick and placed the tip at her opening. Just as I was about to slide in, a wave of guilt hit me.

"Sage, are you sure about this? Because once we do this, it's over between you and him."

Without hesitation, she said, "I'm sure!"

Before she could get the two words out of her mouth, I pushed my way inside.

"Aahh!" she released, as if she had been holding it in.

"Fuck!" I grunted into her neck. Her pussy is tight as hell. There's no fucking way that nigga hittin' it right.

We got into a groove as our strokes began to match each other. Sage has the best pussy, hands down, of any girl I've ever fucked. Wet, I mean, soaking wet, gripping my dick like it was made just for me.

"Shit Sage! You gon' make me a two-minute nigga. This shit feel so damn good."

Her legs are now on my shoulders and I'm going deep. I pulled my dick all the way out to the tip and pushed it back in repeatedly.

"Brees, ummhmm baby! Shit this feel good. I cummmiiinnn baabbyy!"

"I'm right behind you!" I said as I shot my seeds inside of her, not caring about the fact that I wasn't wearing a condom or whether or not she is on birth control.

We were both spent, breathing like we'd just run a marathon. Lifting my body from hers, I laid next to her and pulled her close to me.

"No turning back now Sage. It's me and you," I said, looking into her eyes.

"I know. It should have always been you," she whispered and kissed my lips. "It's always been you. I just didn't---"

"Sshh. Let's not do this tonight," I kissed her forehead and held her until we both fell asleep.

We awoke to someone frantically ringing the doorbell and banging on the door simultaneously. Reaching for my phone, I saw that it was ten in the morning.

"Who the fuck?" I said to myself, as I got out of my bed and grabbed some shorts.

"What's going on?" Sage sat up and yawned.

"I don't know. Stay here though."

When I got to my front door, I yanked the door open and Zane pushed his way in.

"The fuck is yo problem nigga?" I grabbed him before he could get too far.

"Why the fuck is Sage's car parked in front of your house nigga?" He got in my face.

"Because she's upstairs. Get the fuck outta my face!" I pushed him towards the front door but he wasn't going. Zane and I were the same height, but I had a little more weight on me. I hope I don't have to knock his ass out.

"Why is my bitch here Brees? You fuckin' my girl?" Zane angrily questioned me.

"Naw nigga, he's fucking your EX girl!" Sage yelled from the top of the stairs.

Zane looked in the direction of Sage's voice and if looks could kill, Sage would be as good as gone.

"This is what the fuck you on Sage. You fuckin' the homie? Wow, I didn't know you got down like that."

"Fuck you Zane. How many times have you cheated on me since we've been together? Don't try to make me seem like I'm some kinda hoe," Sage yelled from the top of the stairs.

"I ain't makin' it seem like shit. You fuckin' my best friend. You a hoe!" he spat back at her.

Before I could stop myself, I punched Zane in his jaw. Yeah, it was a cheap shot and he wasn't ready but I wasn't about to stand there and let him disrespect Sage like that when he's the one that's been fucking up all along.

"What the fuck?" Zane said as he stumbled back, holding his jaw. "Oh, it's like that nigga," he continued before he charged me.

I lost my footing and fell to the floor and Zane was on top of me. He landed a few blows to my head before I was able to flip him over and land a few hits to his body. I could hear Sage screaming in the background. When we were both back on our feet, Sage forced her way between us before either of us were able to swing again.

"Cut this shit out!" She turned and faced Zane. "There's no reason to fight. We are done! I gave you too many chances to get your shit together but last night was the last straw. I heard you fucking that bitch and I'm not foolish enough to keep letting you fuck me over," she yelled in his face.

"Hell yeah we done. I don't share pussy. You can have this bitch!" Zane looked at Sage with nothing but rage in his eyes. Then he shook his head at me. I moved to hit him again but Sage stopped me.

"No, baby. He's not even worth it," she tried to calm me.

"Baby? How long you been fuckin' my girl, Brees? I knew your ass was jealous of me. Always have been," he said with a look of disgust on his face.

"Nigga I've never been jealous of your ass. And this is some shit that just happened. Now get the fuck out!" I demanded as I walked to my front door.

"That's cool. You can have my leftovers," he looked Sage up and down and you could see the hate radiating from his face.

Luckily, he left without further incidence. After I locked up, Sage and I went back upstairs to my bedroom. We sat on my bed, facing each other. She looked sad.

"Are you sure about this? I mean, it's too late now. My friendship with Zane is done. And I'm not saying you aren't worth it because you are. I just need to know if this is what you really want?" I held her hands in mine and looked into her eyes as I spoke.

"I don't want you to think badly of me when I tell you this," she began.

"Oh shit!" I joked.

"No seriously Brees. Just listen," she paused briefly. "Do you remember the day that I met Zane?" I nodded. "It was you, Zane, his brother Zach, and Shannon. When you guys approached me and Lisa, I was hoping you'd be the one that wanted to talk to me. But you were quiet and didn't say much. Shannon was talking to Lisa and they hit it off. Since you didn't say anything, I gave Zane my number when he asked. But you were the one I wanted to be giving my number to," she confessed, nervously.

"Yeah. But Sage, you've been with Zane for over a year. I know you weren't with him all this time and didn't want to be."

"But I was. Don't get me wrong. I fell for Zane, maybe even loved him at some point. He was perfect in the beginning. But after about three months, I knew he was cheating. I had no evidence but my gut told me that he was. I honestly didn't care because every time he and I had sex, I pretended that I was making love to you. My days and nights have been filled with fantasies about being with you. Zane was fun to hang out with, when he wasn't on no bullshit. But every time I close my eyes, I see myself with you."

"Why didn't you just break up with him?" I questioned.

"Because then I would never get to see you. Staying with him was my only way to be around you."

"You know what you just told me is fucked up right? If you weren't feeling him, you should have moved the fuck on Sage!" I raised my voice but I wasn't yelling.

"I didn't say I wasn't feeling him. My feelings for him grew but I couldn't get you out of my mind. I never stopped wanting to be with you instead of him," Sage acknowledged. "I can't help how I feel Brees!"

I got up and began to pace in front of her. My feelings for Sage are strong, I can't deny that. But now I'm wondering if she planned this whole thing. The first time she contacted me about Zane, I wondered where she got my number but I didn't put a lot of thought into it. She started off sending a text every couple of days, asking about Zane's whereabouts. Before long, she'd text me just to see what I was doing. Next, she would call and we'd talk on the phone for a few minutes and it escalated from there. It had gotten to the point that we communicated every day, whether it was texting or talking on the phone.

A few times I ended up at her crib or her at mine. That's when I knew I was beginning to have feelings for her. It was solidified when we took it too far and I ended up using my fingers to bring her to a climax.

"What are you thinking Brees?" Sage broke the silence.

"I honestly don't know what to think. I just fucked up a ten-year friendship and I'm starting to think that you planned all of this," I calmly stated.

"Are you serious right now?" she yelled. "I didn't plan to fall in love with my boyfriend's best friend. Who the fuck does that?" She stood from the bed and picked her clothes up from the floor, marched into the bathroom, then slammed and locked the door.

I let out a deep breath and fell back on my bed. "Shit!"

A few minutes later, Sage stormed out of the bathroom fully dressed, causing me to sit up. She didn't look my way as she put on her Nike slides.

"I'm sorry I ruined your friendship but I thought that what I felt for you was reciprocated. I'm sure if you talk to Zane ya'll will be homies again. You don't have to worry about me getting in the way," she had tears streaming down her face and her lips trembled.

"What do you mean?" I asked.

"I mean just what I said!" She walked out of my bedroom and possibly, out of my life.

"FUUCCCKKK!"

****

The last five months went by in a blur. Zane and I are still not on good terms. We found ourselves in the same place a few times and the tension was thick. I didn't say shit to him and he didn't say shit to me, although he threw a lot of shade with some of the comments he made. I refused to acknowledge him or his comments with his petty ass.

I miss the hell outta Sage. I've driven by her house more times than I can count. I've been stalking her social media pages. I look at her name in my contacts daily but I never call or text. So much time has gone by now that I'm sure she probably doesn't want shit to do with me. But what she confessed to me that day had me all fucked up. On one hand, it seems as if she intentionally seduced me and I fell right into her trap. On the other hand, the connection we had was strong and I can't deny my feelings for her.

It's taken me a minute to recognize what my feelings are for Sage. I've been low-key depressed about this situation and I have no idea what to do and no one to talk to about it.

I'm at home, chilling in my den and received a text message from an unknown number.

Unknown: You need to check on Sage.

Me: Who is this?

Unknown: Lisa.

Me: How'd you get my number?

Unknown: Not important just check on Sage please.

I contemplated briefly. "It's only seven. I guess it's not too late," I said to myself as I went to grab my things to leave.

On the way over to Sage's place, I had a million things going through my mind. *Why would I need to check on her? Is she sick? Did something happen? Is she safe?* I guess I'll find out when I get there.

Sage lived in a townhouse in a nice subdivision about twenty minutes from me. I decided to park a couple of houses down, just in case she looked outside and saw my car and refused to answer the door.

I walked up to her door, rang the doorbell, and stepped to the side a bit so she wouldn't see me in the little window near the door.

Just as I was about to ring the doorbell again, I heard the locks on the door. Sage was talking as she opened the door.

"Lisa, why didn't you just use your key? You know it's hard for me to get up from that soft ass couch!" she fussed and turned right around and went the other way. *Damn, her ass looks fatter.* I stepped in, closed and locked the door. Sage still didn't know that it was me and not Lisa.

"Sage!" I called out to her. She screamed and turned around simultaneously.

"Fuck Brees! What are you doing here? You scared the shit out of me," she held onto the wall that was near her with one hand and held her stomach with the other.

"You're pregnant?" I questioned.

"Dammit!" she whispered.

"Is that my baby?"

"Why are you here Brees?" she ignored my questions.

"Sage, what the fuck is going on? Is that my baby?"

She folded her arms over her chest and they rested on her stomach. She looks so beautiful. Her breasts are fuller, her nose has spread a little bit, along with her hips.

"Does it really matter?" she finally spoke. "You made it clear that you think I'm a sneaky, conniving woman that plotted to ruin you and your best friend's relationship by forcing myself on you. This is MY baby!"

"Sage, baby, that's not what I think. I've missed you so much, baby. I just didn't know what to do. Everyday I've wanted to reach out to you. But---"

"Then why didn't you?" she interrupted me.

"At first, I called myself giving you some time to cool off. Then I let too much time pass and I didn't know what to say. I was trying to sort out my feelings and figure out if what I feel for you is...love. Sage, tell me, is that my baby?"

She looked everywhere but at me. Her eyes began to water and she bit her bottom lip. I took a few steps toward her and she held up her hand.

"Don't! I can't do this with you. You hurt me Brees. More than Zane ever could."

"Baby please, we can work through this. I love you. I swear I do. I just...I've never had these feelings before," I began walking towards her again and this time she didn't stop me. "Give me a chance to show you how much I love you. I've missed you so much."

I grabbed her hands and pulled her close to me. She looked up into my eyes and tears fell from hers like a waterfall.

"Baby please, I'm so sorry. I've driven past here almost every day. I've wanted to call or text but didn't know what to say. I swear, you consumed my every thought," I poured out my heart because I refused to let her go again.

"She's yours," Sage whispered through her tears.

"She? It's a girl?" I smiled down at her.

She nodded. "And before you ask, I hadn't had sex with Zane for a month before we were together and the timeline doesn't line up for it to be his. Besides, we ALWAYS used condoms."

"I wasn't going to ask but thank you for clarifying," I laughed. "Do you forgive me?" I put my arms around her waist and kissed her forehead.

"We are having a baby. We have to get along," she stated.

"I don't want to just get along Sage. I want you to be my woman and one day, when you're ready, my wife."

"Yeah okay," she said, trying to step out of my hold.

"I'm serious Sage," I held her tighter so she couldn't move and she looked back up at me. "From this moment right now, we are together. You are mine and I am yours," I kissed her lips.

It started off as a few pecks and turned passionate. Sage put her arms around my neck and pushed her tongue into my mouth. Her forcefulness caught me by surprise but my dick responded immediately. Sage pulled away from me and yanked me in the direction of her bedroom.

"What are you doing?" I asked as I followed behind her.

"I haven't had sex in five months and this pregnancy got me horny as hell. You're about to give me this dick!"

"Oh shit. Well let's go! I heard pregnant pussy is the best!" I picked her up bridal style and ran to her room.

When we got to her room I put her down. We removed our clothes in a frenzy. She planted herself in the middle of the bed, butt ass naked. I've never seen a more beautiful sight. Her stomach isn't that big but you can tell that she's pregnant.

"Brees, stop staring and bring your ass over here!" Sage demanded.

"Damn baby, you sure have gotten bossy," I teased.

"I'm not bossy, I'm horny," she whined.

I walked over to the bed and grabbed both her legs, pulling her to the edge. Lifting one leg, I planted kisses down the inside, until I reached her mound.

"Brees, you can eat my pussy later. Right now, you need to give me the dick!"

I climbed on top of her, being careful not to put all of my weight on her stomach. In one swift move, I entered her already wet tunnel of sweetness. We both released loud moans.

"I haven't had sex in five months either. This is gonna be quick," I admitted.

I pushed deep inside and her pussy was like a suction. If I died right here, deep inside of Sage's walls, I'd die a happy man with a huge smile stuck on my face. I continued to put in deep strokes and Sage began to lose it.

"Brees, baby you feel soooo good. Oh my gaaa!"

"I need you to cum for me Sage," I commanded and pushed her knees up to her ears.

"I'm close baby," she told me as she matched my strokes. "I'm cummin'," she sang.

"Fuck! Me too," I groaned into her neck. I felt her pussy contracting on my dick and it was wrap. If she wasn't already pregnant she would be now. My release felt like it was never ending.

When my dick stopped contracting, I rolled over the side and Sage snuggled up next to me.

"I love you Brees."

"I love you too. You and our baby girl," I replied, then kissed her forehead.

A few minutes later, Sage had dozed off, leaving me awake with my thoughts. I lost my best friend, which I will admit, is a hard pill to swallow. But I found the love of my life in the process. Maybe, with time, Zane and I will be cool again. Either way, I know I made the right choice.

THE END

2 THINGS AREN'T ALWAYS WHAT THEY SEEM

"Guess what I stumbled upon the other day?" I said to my best friends, Cybil and Kenzie, as we sat down at our table in our favorite restaurant. They looked at me, waiting for me to continue.

"Grayson used my laptop the other day to check his work email and didn't log out," I began.

"And?" they said simultaneously.

"I did a little snooping. I figured since he left it open on my laptop, God was trying to tell me something."

"And?" they repeated.

Just as I began speaking again, the waitress came up and took our drink orders. Once she was gone, I continued.

"Ya'll remember Raquel Simpson, from high school, the one---," I started.

"Yeah, yeah, yeah, we remember her. I mean, who can forget her trifling ass?" Kenzie interrupted.

"I think her and Gray are screwing around," I blurted it and took a deep breath.

It feels so good to finally tell someone. A week ago, when I first saw the emails, I could have died right there. But I want to be sure before I confront my husband. I didn't plan on divulging this information to my girls because I'm so embarrassed but I had to talk to somebody before I completely lost it.

"Oh my God, Harper, why do you think that?" Cybil asked. Kenzie sat there with her mouth open.

"I saw it with my own eyes. They've met up several times, usually during the day but also a couple of times in the evening."

"Have you asked Grayson about it?" Kenzie finally spoke again.

"Is he acting any different?" Cybil asked.

"I haven't said anything and he's acting normal. I don't want to jump the gun. I need concrete evidence before I do something drastic."

The waitress came back to take our order. None of us had looked at the menu yet but since we come here so often, we didn't need to. We placed our orders and were back to our conversation.

"We need a plan so we can catch his ass in the act!" Kenzie exclaimed. She is a pro at this type of stuff. Unfortunately, she's been unlucky in love one too many times and caught a few of her cheating boyfriends in the act.

"Do you still have access to his email?" Cybil inquired, as if she was pondering something.

"I do. The last email that he sent was confirming a meeting for tomorrow morning. It's Saturday and he knows that I usually meet up with my mom to go to the Farmer's Market."

"Okay," Kenzie said. I could tell that she is formulating a plan. "Cancel your plans with your mom. Make sure you tell her that you're planning a surprise for Grayson and not to tell him you guys canceled. What time is Grayson supposed to meet Raquel?"

"Noon," I replied, sullenly.

"Good. Leave out as you normally would to meet your mom and come to my place. Wait! Do you know where they are meeting?" Kenzie asked.

"Yep! At the Holiday Inn on Central Blvd."

"Damn Harper, his ass is really cheating. At least he ain't spending all ya'll money on fancy hotels!" Cybil interjected.

"Cybil! Stop being so insensitive. This is serious," Kenzie reprimanded.

But Cybil is right. My husband is meeting another woman at a hotel and has been doing so on a regular basis. *What else could they be meeting for?*

"Anyway, Harper, you come to my house and Cybil you go and park at the hotel. When they get there, I want you to discreetly follow them inside and find out what room they are in," Kenzie continued sharing her plan.

"I can do that," Cybil assured us.

"Then you're going to text us and we will meet you there so we can fuck their asses up!" Kenzie whisper shouted and banged her fist on the table.

The waitress came with our food and we ate as Kenzie ironed out the rest of the details of the plan. I guess I should say they ate. I no longer had an appetite.

****

Saturday morning arrived and I followed through with the plan. Grayson was especially attentive before I left out to "meet my mom." I could barely stand for him to touch me but I think I played it off pretty well.

When I got to Kenzie's house, she had made breakfast and mimosas. I still didn't have an appetite but I ate a little so that I would have some energy. I passed on the mimosas though. I could tell that Kenzie didn't want to bring up the real reason why I was there until it was time for us to leave for the hotel. I was thankful for that because I didn't feel like talking about it. The text from Cybil came and I almost vomited.

"I can't believe this nigga is really cheating on me. All this time, I thought we had the perfect marriage. He hasn't given me any signs that he's unhappy. How could he do this to me?" I cried to Kenzie. She hugged me and rubbed my back but her words were not consoling.

"Because men are assholes Harper. I thought Grayson was different and you had gotten lucky but clearly, he's just like the rest of them." I got another text from Cybil just as she finished her rant.

Cyb: Change of plans. They didn't go inside of the hotel. He got in her car and they are headed south.

I told Kenzie what she said so we pulled over to wait for further instructions.

"What the fuck is he doing with her ratchet ass? I mean, if he's gonna cheat, he couldn't upgrade?" Kenzie said.

"There is no upgrade from me so why even try."

"I heard that bestie!" she laughed, giving me a high-five.

We both scrolled our social media pages while we waited for Cybil to tell us where to go. Finally, another text from her came through.

Cyb: They parked and went inside of a house. The address is 2361 Spruce Lane.

I told Kenzie and put the address in the GPS. She broke all of the speed limit laws but we made it there safely, driving past the house and parking a few houses up, behind Cybil's car. We all got out and walked towards the house.

"I don't want to alarm them. So I'm going to ring the doorbell but as soon as she opens the door, I'm beating her ass," I said very calmly.

"What about him? He's the one you should be beating!" Cybil expressed.

"Cybil shut up! Damn! Let her do what she wants," Kenzie declared.

"She's right! He's the one that owes me his loyalty," I agreed with Cybil.

I came ready to fight, wearing leggings, gym shoes, and no jewelry except for my wedding ring. It's three carats and I figured it would benefit me to keep it on.

I rang the doorbell once. My heart was racing as I waited. I rang the doorbell again and folded my arms across my chest. My hands were sweaty and my ears started to ring.

"Fuck this!" Kenzie yelled and started banging on the door.

The door was yanked open and Raquel and Grayson stood there, surprised, to say the least.

"What the hell?" Raquel said.

"Harper, what are you doing here?" Grayson said, confused.

Before he finished the question, I pounced on him, making him stumble backwards. All of the anger I'd been holding in for the past week and a half came out. I threw punch after punch, as he tried to restrain me.

"Harper! What the fuck is your problem baby? Calm down!" Grayson shouted.

"Don't tell me to calm down! How could you Gray? I trusted you and this is how you repay me. I hate you!" I yelled as I continued swinging my fists.

He was finally able to grab my fist and pull me close to his chest.

"Harper, what are you talking about baby?" he asked.

"How could you cheat on me? I love you and I gave you my heart and you fuckin' cheat on me with this nasty bitch,"

"Excuse me!" I heard Raquel say behind me.

"Shut up hoe!" Kenzie spat.

"Cheat on you? Baby, I am not cheating on you!"

I had calmed down enough that Grayson moved me away from his chest to look at my face, although he held my arms close to my body.

"I saw the emails Gray. I saw all of the times you met up with her. Don't lie now!" I cried and tried to remove myself from his hold.

"Baby, I swear to you, I'm not lying,"

"Then why have you been seeing this sneaky ass bitch!" I yanked away from him.

"I'm not gon' be too many more bitches and hoes around here!" Raquel spoke up.

"You gon' be whatever the fuck I say you are!" I said, yanking away from Grayson and walking towards her. Grayson snatched me back real quick before I was able to put my hands on Raquel.

"Harper! Let me explain! I am not sleeping with Raquel. She's a realtor and she's helping me find a house. I wanted to surprise you. I would never cheat on you, baby. I thought you would want a bigger place with the baby coming."

"BABY?!" Cybil and Kenzie said at the same time.

I turned around to see the shocked expressions on Cybil and Kenzie's faces.

"You're pregnant?" they both said.

"Umm, my bad. Did I forget to tell ya'll?" I replied innocently.

They both rushed over to me. "Harper, why didn't you tell us?" Kenzi asked.

"I don't know. I just wanted to wait until I knew everything was okay," I replied. After suffering from a miscarriage six months ago, Grayson and I decided we'd keep the pregnancy to ourselves until after the three month mark.

"How far along are you?" Cybil asked.

"Just made thirteen weeks yesterday," I expressed excitedly as Grayson wrapped his arms around me from behind.

"Awww, congratulations bestie. I'm so happy for you," Cybil said, hugging both me and Grayson.

"Ahem...I think I deserve an apology," Raquel said from the other side of the room.

We all turned in her direction. I hesitated briefly and Grayson gave me a nudge.

"Baby, you know you were wrong coming up in here ready for war. Raquel was just doing her job," Grayson reasoned with me.

"Ughh....you're right," I said to Grayson. "Raquel, I apologize for barging in here ready to beat your ass and making assumptions. Thank you for helping him find this beautiful house. I still don't like your ass but –"

"Harper!" Grayson yelled. I looked at him and shrugged my shoulders.

"I guess that's good enough. Grayson, if you want this house, you guys can come to my office on Monday to start the paperwork," Raquel walked towards the door. "I normally don't do this but feel free to keep the keys and bring them Monday. I'll let you give her a tour." With that, she walked out, gently closing the door behind her.

"Harper, I think you hurt her feelings," Kenzie laughed.

"I apologized. What more does she want?" I said, dismissively.

"You could have left off the end. But enough about that, let me show you the house," Grayson took my hand and pulled me along. Cybil and Kenzi followed.

****

A month and a half later, we moved into our new home. My pregnancy is going well and I'm almost twenty weeks along. Grayson hired a moving company because he didn't want me doing anything. All of our furniture is in place and my girls, Cybil and Kenzi, are here to help me unpack. Grayson has been a little overbearing for this pregnancy but I won't complain. Losing our first baby was tough for the both of us.

"I can't believe that you and Grayson are now homeowners and about to be somebody's parents. I'm so excited for you two!" Cybil gushed. "We have to start planning for your baby shower. And oh my gosh, are you guys gonna have a housewarming."

"Damn Cyb, slow down. They aren't the first people we know to do this you know," Kenzie snapped. She must be fighting with her flavor of the month boo. She's been super cranky lately.

"But they are the first in our close circle and I'm excited for them. What's your problem?" Cybil snapped back.

"Nothing, I'm good. Harper this box says shoes. Not sure why it's in here. I'll go put it in your room," Kenzie picked up the box and went towards my bedroom.

"What's been up with her lately? Has she said anything to you?" I asked Cybil once Kenzie was out of earshot.

"I have no idea and she hasn't mentioned anything. But her attitude is annoying."

"Maybe she's having man problems. Remember she was kinda getting serious about the one dude, the one with the freckles," I recalled.

"I don't know but I'm gonna cuss her ass out if she keeps giving me attitude for no damn reason," Cybil fussed.

"I'm gonna go talk to her. You have absolutely no patience Cybil, I swear," I shook my head at her and went to find Kenzie in my bedroom.

When I walked into my room, I saw the box that Kenzie had but I didn't see Kenzie. I walked in a little further and I heard voices coming from the walk-in closet.

"What the fuck is your problem Kenzie?" I heard what I knew to be Grayson's voice.

"How can you just fuck me like that and just move on?" Kenzie replied.

Wait! What?

"Kenzie, it was a one night stand! That's what happens. We both knew that shit when it happened. Why do you keep bringing this shit up?" Grayson said, sounding frustrated.

"Because you weren't supposed to move on with one of my best friends."

"I didn't know she was your best friend. I didn't even know you. I knew I should have just told her right away. I thought you were cool when you convinced me that it was best to forget it ever happened. I forgot it ever happened as soon as I left. Clearly you didn't," Grayson whispered yelled.

"I can't forget it Grayson. I've tried. It was the best sex that I've ever had. I thought we had a connection," Kenzie confessed.

"Well for me, it was exactly what I meant it to be. We hooked up once. I didn't ask for your number, I didn't find you on social media, I didn't even know your last name until I was with Harper. I didn't think about you anymore after that night, Kenzie. I'm sorry if it meant more to you than it did to me. I love my wife so you need to let this shit go!"

"You never think about me and you being married and having a baby. This could be us," she said, lowly.

"Are you fuckin' crazy? This could not be us. It was never going to be us. What else can I say to you to get you to understand that I didn't and don't want to be with you. It was one fucking time!" Grayson's voice began elevate.

I couldn't take it anymore. I walked into the closet, Kenzie's back was to me as she looked up at Grayson with her arms folded across her chest. Grayson saw me and his eyes got wide. I'm sure the look on my face let him know that I heard everything and that I was ready to fuck shit up. I yanked Kenzie by her ponytail and she was caught by surprise.

"Ouch!" she screamed and put her hands up to her head.

"You little bitch!" I yelled. Before I could do any more damage, Grayson grabbed me.

"Harper, the baby!" he hollered.

Yes, for a moment, I completely forgot that I was pregnant.

"Kenzie I think you should go!" Grayson held me with one hand and pointed to the door with the other.

"Oh hell naw. Ya'll got some explaining to do," I yanked my hand away from Grayson's and went and stood in front of our bedroom door. "No one's leaving until ya'll tell me what the fuck I just overheard."

Grayson came to me and took my hands in his. "Look baby, before you and I met, Kenzie and I had a one night stand. A few months later, I met you. Once we became exclusive, you introduced me to your friends. Honestly, it had been at least six months and I didn't recognize Kenzie until she reminded me that we already knew each other and how. I didn't think it was a big deal. I ---"

"You didn't think it was a big deal that you had fucked my friend, Grayson?"

"It was one time before I knew you baby. By the time I found out you were friends, I had already fallen in love with you. I wasn't about to give you up for a random fuck!" He released one of my hands and pointed to Kenzie.

"Wow Grayson! Just wow!" Kenzie said in disbelief.

He let my other hand go and turned towards Kenzie. "What the fuck do you want me to say. I love my wife. I slept with you one fuckin' time before I knew my wife. Every time you bring this shit up I tell you the same thing. It meant nothing!"

I stepped in front of Grayson and he pulled me back. "I'm not gon' beat this bitch like I should. But she better hope I don't see her ass after I have this baby." I gave her the side-eye then turned back to Grayson. "She's not the only one in the wrong here Gray. You both should have told me that you had a history. But you," I said, turning to Kenzie and poking her on the shoulder with my index finger, "you're supposed to be my best friend. You should have told me immediately. You owed that to me more than he did at the time."

"But I didn't---," Kenzie started.

"I'm not done talking bitch. Shut the fuck up! Instead of telling me that your hoe ass had a one night stand with the dude I was dating, you go behind my back and hold it over his head. What did you think would happen Kenzie? Did you think you would wear him down and he would fuck your loose pussy ass again?"

She stood there, saying nothing, shaking her leg.

"You don't have anything to say now?" I paused, waiting for an answer. She said nothing. "Get the fuck out of my house and out of my life Kenzie. I'm so done with your hoe ass!"

She quickly brushed past us, with tears in her eyes. I went and sat on my bed and put my head in my hands. This is all too much to process. I felt Grayson sit on the bed next to me.

"Baby, I--"

"Don't! I don't wanna hear shit from you right now Grayson!"

"But baby--"

"Not now Grayson! Just...I can't right now. I need a minute."

He got up and took a couple of steps but stopped and got on his knees in front of me.

"I'm not giving you a minute. I need you to hear me right now. I'm not walking away and letting this shit fester any longer than it should. We're about to fix this right now."

He paused and I didn't say a word. The forcefulness in his tone turned me on and my pussy began to throb.

"I'm sorry baby. I know I should have told you. But I can't stress to you how little it meant to me. It was one time baby. ONE TIME, before you and I met. Before I fell in love with you. Before you became my wife and the mother of my child. I shouldn't have let her convince me that she could let it go. I was wrong and I'm sorry."

"I'm so pissed at you right now," I pushed him away, got up and paced back and forth. "Not because you slept with her. We didn't know each other when it happened, so it's whatever. But you've kept this secret from me for so long, Gray. Especially when she started trying to use it as leverage."

"Harper, baby, she was never gonna convince me to sleep with her again. I guess that's why it wasn't a big deal to me. I love you so much and I knew telling you would hurt and that it would be the end of your friendship with Kenzie. I didn't want to be the reason that happened."

"You weren't worried about me leaving you?" He was still on his knees and I stopped in front of him.

"Hell naw, we in this shit for life!" he exclaimed confidently before continuing. "I knew you'd be upset with me. But I'm not letting you go, for anything or anyone, ever," he lifted my t-shirt dress and kissed my belly. "We in this forever baby."

"What the hell is going on?" Cybil said, startling both me and Grayson. "Oh my bad. I didn't mean to interrupt. What's up with Kenzie? She just rushed outta here upset and crying."

"Let me ask you something," I said quietly as I took slow but determined steps towards Cybil.

"What's up?" she asked.

"Have you slept with Grayson?" I asked with folded arms across my chest.

"What?" Grayson and Cybil yelled at the same time.

"Are you seriously asking me that?" Cybil asked as if I offended her.

"Harper, don't do this," Grayson reasoned.

"I'm waiting for an answer," I said.

"No! I have not slept with Grayson. Why would you---wait, is that why Kenzie left crying? Grayson, you dirty ass nigga. How could you?" she walked towards Grayson and pushed him in the chest.

I went back to my bed and sat on the edge. I don't really think that Cybil and Grayson have ever slept together but I had to ask. I didn't think he and Kenzie had either but I was wrong about that.

"Hold up Cybil. Don't make assumptions before you know the whole story." He then proceeded to tell her everything that I now know. I didn't care to hear it again but I wanted to make sure he didn't change up his story.

"Wow! This is crazy," Cybil expressed her disbelief. She came and sat next to me on the bed and put her arm around my shoulders.

"Harper, I promise you I had no idea. Kenzie never said anything to me about having a one night stand with Grayson. I can't believe --- well, actually I can. You know that's how she rolls. But it was before you and Grayson met."

"I know that and that's not my issue. My issue is that they kept it from me for damn near two years. Not to mention that she's been trying to convince him to fuck her again," I explained.

"You lyin'? Damn, that's so damn triflin'. I would have never thought she'd do something like that," Cybil shook her head.

"Cybil, I'm not trying to be rude. Thank you for your help today. But I need to talk to my wife," Grayson said.

"Is that your way of asking me to leave?" she looked at Grayson and he nodded. "Harper, you good? If you want me to stay, I will."

"I'm good. I'll call you tomorrow," I assured her. She gave me a hug and left.

As soon as we heard the front door close, Grayson was back on his knees in front of me.

"Baby, I swear I didn't keep it from you on no sneaky type shit. I know it seems that way but I'm telling the truth. I would never do anything to hurt you intentionally. I kept it from you for the sake of your friendship with her, that's it."

"You know, when I think back, I realize that Kenzie has never really been for our relationship. I just assumed it was because she's always been bitter towards men. She's been that way for as long as I can remember, so her attitude about you didn't come as a surprise. It's like she was waiting for us to fail. When we moved in together, she said it was too soon. When you proposed, she said we were rushing. When I told them that I thought you were cheating on me with Raquel, she was all too eager to cook up a plan to catch you in the act. Following you was all her idea," I rambled on as everything started to come together in my head.

"But lately," I continued, "since you surprised me with the house and I told them about the baby, she's been extremely irritable and more attitudinal than normal. Cybil noticed it too and wanted to check her about it but I kept telling her to let it go."

"I'm just gon' be honest baby. I don't really care about any of that. I mean, I'm glad that you can see that she was hatin' on you and our relationship. If you want to still be friends with her, it's cool. I understand that you've been friends with her for a very long time. I just need you to know that there has never been anything between Kenzie and I and there never will be. She is not a threat to what we have, no one is. All I want is for you to forgive me. That's my one and only concern," Grayson pleaded and kissed the back of both of my hands.

"If you ever keep a secret like this from me again---," I started before Grayson interrupted me.

"I won't baby. No more secrets. You have my word," he hugged me and brushed his lips across my cheek. "I love you too much to lose you over some bullshit, especially mediocre pussy."

We both laughed and his lips found mine. I allowed him to explore my mouth with his tongue briefly before I pulled away.

"I'm still mad but I forgive you," I paused for a second. "And don't you ever mention her or another bitch's pussy in my presence again."

He laughed before replying. "Duly noted. But I don't want you to be mad anymore," Grayson said and began lifting the hem of the t-shirt dress again.

"Stop Gray! You can't have no pussy. You're grounded," I smacked his hand away.

"Oh, you not gon' give me none of MY pussy, Harper?" he continued pushing my dress up.

"Nope! I told you that I'm still mad. Now stop!" I tried to be firm and moved away from him to the center of the bed. He came right along with me, gently pushed me back and hovered over me.

"But baby, I said I was sorry," he pouted as he looked into my eyes. There hasn't been a single time since we've been together that I've denied him. Today would be no different and I'm certain he knew that.

"You want me to beg baby?" he pecked, then sucked my bottom lip into his mouth. "I don't mind begging," he nibbled on my ear then moved to my neck. "Please, baby. I want some of my good, good."

I tried to keep my legs closed but my body contradicted my mind. Grayson easily nudge his way in between them, which caused my dress to hike up to my waist. He used one hand to move the crotch of my panties to the side then rubbed his fingers across my already slick opening.

"Why you telling me no, Harper? My pussy is telling me that she's ready," Grayson whispered.

He pushed one, then two fingers into my throbbing hole and I let out a soft moan.

"I know you want this dick. I don't know why you tried to fight it baby," he teased.

"Just shut up and give it to me!" I demanded.

He removed his fingers, licking the juices from one finger and putting the other in my mouth for me to do the same. I sat up so that he could remove my dress and bra. Grayson barely gave me a chance to lay back down before he removed my underwear. I grabbed the hem of his shirt, letting him know that I wanted it off. He stood next to the bed and was naked in seconds.

"Turn around and get on your knees," he commanded. I did as he said and prepared myself for his entry. But it wasn't his dick that I felt, it was his tongue.

"Oh shit!" I called out in surprise.

His thick, wide tongue swiped up and down my slit while he fingered me. Since being pregnant, my hormone levels are through the roof and just breathing on my pussy will have me cumming like Niagara Falls in seconds.

"Damn baby! I'm about to cum!" I grinded my pelvic area against his face, I'm sure he damn near suffocated. My orgasm came like a Tsunami and I almost collapsed.

"Naw baby. You can't tap out yet," Grayson teased and held me up.

Before I could get my head together, Gray entered me from behind.

"Fuck baby!" I screamed.

"You told me to give you the dick so I'm giving you the dick!"

That he was! His strokes were going deep as hell. But I wasn't about to let him out fuck me so I threw my ass back and matched his strokes.

"Oh you trying to make me bust this nut real quick huh. I gotchu. Keep poppin' that pussy on this dick," Grayson taunted.

His strokes became methodical and I was barely hanging on. My knees buckled but I'm going to snatch this nut out of him before I let that happen. I squeezed my walls so tight and the dick felt amazing.

"Baby, please. I'm cummin'!" I belted out. My pussy pulsed and I exploded.

"Aghh got dammit baby!" he said through clenched teeth just as I felt his dick began to throb and he released his seeds inside of me. He pulled out and my knees and arms gave out. I crashed on the bed and it was lights out.

Grayson swung my legs around so that I could be in the middle of the bed and cleaned me up with a warm towel before crawling into bed next to me with a blanket. He pulled me close to him, with my back to his chest and kissed my temple.

"Baby, you still mad?"

"Shut up Grayson!"

THE END

3 LOVE DOESN'T HURT

Tonight could be fun! It's always better when we go on double dates. It takes some of the pressure away from me. The other couple usually keeps him distracted enough to not focus too much on what I'm doing or saying wrong. As long as I don't talk too much, or eat too much, or drink too much, or laugh too much, tonight could be fun.

"Shayla, are you ready yet? Damn!" Kurt yelled, barging into our bedroom.

"Just about. Let me grab my shoes," I replied, keeping my voice nice and even so that he wouldn't think I was raising my voice.

I walked out of our walk-in closet with my heels in my hand. Kurt looked at me from his position on the bed and sprang up.

"Where the fuck do you think you're goin' lookin' like a hoe? Take that shit off and find something more presentable! You can't do shit right," he shouted and stomped out of our bedroom, slamming the door. "And hurry the fuck up!" he added.

I'm wearing a red, mid-thigh, fitted, short-sleeve dress. I purposely chose this dress because he said we were going to a club after dinner. The dress isn't too revealing, aside from being short, and I planned to wear a denim jacket over it so that my arms wouldn't be exposed.

It doesn't matter what I wear, Kurt will still find something wrong with it. Anytime that he takes me out, which isn't often, I have to change clothes at least three times. I should have been prepared for this but I thought that for once, I could get it right the first time.

I let out a huge sigh and walked back into our closet, admiring all of the clothes he spoiled me with that he never allowed me to wear. The only reason I had most of this shit is because buying me things is his way of apologizing.

This time, I decided on a black, quarter-sleeve, fitted dress that went just below my knees, and my leopard heels, still pairing with my denim jacket. The outfit seems safe enough but you just never know with Kurt. I left the bedroom and walked towards the stairs. Kurt is pacing back and forth in the entryway.

"Why the hell are you standing there like you're stupid? We're already late because of your dumbass, now let's go!" Kurt hollered up at me. *Because I figured you'd make me change again.*

I quickly made my way down the winding staircase, with my heels in hand, putting them on when I got near the door. Kurt stood there holding the door open, allowing me to leave first. I guess this outfit is more to his liking. *Asshole!*

"When we get to this restaurant, I want you to be on your best behavior. Don't do or say no stupid shit!" he warned.

The ride to the restaurant was quiet. I didn't have shit to say to him and he rarely had anything to say to me unless he wanted to make me feel like shit. We pulled up to the valet and he opened my door. Kurt got out, took the ticket from the guy and put his elbow out for me to grab ahold. It took me a moment to intertwine my arm with his because this is some new shit.

He must have noticed the confused look on my face because he said, "I do know how to be a gentlemen. You just don't deserve it."

I wanted to roll my eyes but that my set him off. When we reached the hostess, Kurt did all the talking. Our party had already arrived so she led us to the table.

"Hey man, glad you could make it!" the guy at the table said as he stood and gave Kurt a man hug and some dap. "You don't look like you've aged a bit since we last saw each other, what, like ten years ago."

"You're too kind man! But yeah, I think it was about that long ago. This is Shayla, my beautiful wife and the reason why I look so good. She takes good care of me. Shayla, this is Darius. We went to high school together." *Wife? Since when nigga?*

I finally looked up at the man and could have passed out right there. *Oh my God! This is bad! This is all bad!*

"Hello, Darius. Nice to meet you!" I offered a slight smile as I put my hand out to shake his. Instead, he grabbed my hand and pulled me into a hug. My body tensed and I knew not to hug him back. Somehow, Kurt will turn this hug into me flirting with Darius.

"None of that handshake stuff Shayla, I like hugs. It's good to meet you too," he said, releasing me. "Kurt, you didn't tell me you got married."

Darius returned to his seat, keeping his eyes on me. I waited to see where Kurt sat before I did the same. The table is square and they sat across from each other, while I sat in between them.

"You know how it is man. We ain't got no papers but she's wifey," Kurt paused. "I thought this was a double date. Is your lady in the bathroom?"

"I'm not as lucky with love as you are, man. I'm now single as a dollar bill," Darius stated. "Ya'll planning on making it official anytime soon?"

"Shit, that was quick. I just saw you with a fine ass shorty on your Facebook page not too long ago. You're a dumbass if you fucked that up. She was nice!" Kurt said, as if I wasn't sitting there and completely dodging Darius's question.

"Yeah, she was nice to look at, although she's no Shayla. Don't let this one get away," Darius winked at me.

Kurt looked at me and I shifted in my seat. Thankfully, the waitress came to take our drink orders. The guys ordered themselves some kind of alcoholic drink, while Kurt ordered me a strawberry lemonade.

"You're not drinking tonight Shayla. Surely you can handle something stronger than lemonade," Darius smirked.

"Shayla doesn't drink. She's a good girl," Kurt said, before I could answer.

Naw nigga, I do drink. You just don't let me.

"Is that right? Interesting." Darius rubbed his beard, never taking his eyes off me.

"You know babe, since his date wasn't able to come, why don't I just head home? You guys can hang out and Darius can drop you off later," I suggested.

I need to get out of here. If Darius keeps giving me these lustful looks, tonight is not going to end well for me.

"No, please stay," Darius quickly nixed that idea. "I don't want to run you off just because I can't keep a woman."

I looked at Kurt and the look on his face let me know that I'm already in trouble.

"You know damn well I'm not lettin' your ass drive my car. Don't be stupid," Kurt spat.

"I'm sorry. I just thought you guys would have a more enjoyable night without me tagging along," I apologized, looking down at my hands that were in my lap. I hate when he talks to me like that in public.

Darius reached over and lifted my chin with his finger. "I'm enjoying your company. No need to leave on my account, sweetheart."

"Aye man, I'm gon' need you to keep your hands to yourself and her name is Shalya, not sweetheart!" Kurt pushed Darius's hand away and pulled my chair closer to his.

"My bad man. I don't want her to feel like she needs to leave," Darius apologized.

"Don't worry about how she feels!" Kurt fumed.

With perfect timing again, the waitress came with our drinks and to take our order. I wasn't ready so the guys ordered their food first and just as I was about to tell her what I wanted, Kurt ordered for me, once again. *A goddamn salad nigga!*

Darius could see the frustration on my face and looked back and forth between me and Kurt before he asked, "Damn man, she can't order for herself?"

"Naw, I know what she likes," Kurt said, grabbing and rubbing my hand. I'm assuming that this gesture was meant to be romantic. However, Kurt's touch began making me nauseous long ago.

Clearing my throat, I began to scoot my chair back. "I'm gonna go to the bathroom."

I started to stand but Kurt squeezed my hand real tight and yanked my arm. I sat back down

"Kurt, I need to use the bathroom," I told him.

"Don't be all fuckin' day in there and make me have to come looking for you," he spoke through clenched teeth, squeezing my hand so tight that my eyes began to water.

I nodded and stood again. I could feel Darius's eyes on me but I didn't dare look his way. After a few steps, I could hear Darius's voice.

"What the fuck is up with you man? You treat that woman like shit!" Darius said.

I didn't hear Kurt's response but I'm sure it was nothing but a bunch of bullshit. After asking a hostess, I found the bathroom near the front of the restaurant. As I walked past the entrance, I imagined myself making a run for it. *But where would I go?*

When I walked into the bathroom, I couldn't help but notice how nice it was. Each stall was equipped with a sink and of course, a toilet, and even a small bench inside. *Impressive!*

After handling my business, I walked out of the stall and right into a hard chest, pushing me back into the stall and slamming the door shut. Initially, I didn't see who it was, so I automatically thought it was Kurt on some bullshit.

Before I could protest, my back was against the wall, his lips are on mine and he shoved his tongue into my mouth. His lips are soft and plump. I could taste a trace of whatever liquor he had been drinking. Our tongues made circles around each other's and I allowed myself to get lost.

His lips moved down and went back and forth between my ear and my neck, two of my most sensitive spots. *He remembers!* He lifted my dress above my waist and ripped my thongs off with one hand, while releasing his dick from his pants with the other. Not once did he stop devouring me with his mouth.

I felt his fingers brush against my clit, testing its wetness. He's not disappointed. In one swift move, he is inside of me and I let out a moan. With my legs wrapped around his waist, he pumped inside of me, hard, fast, and deep.

"Fuck, Shayla, you feel just like I remember baby," Darius whispered.

"What are you doing to me?! Shit! I'm about to cum!" I mumbled into his neck.

Just as I climaxed, Darius pulled out and released in his hand. Suddenly, reality set in and I went into panic mode.

"What the fuck are you doing in here?" I pushed him away and quickly grabbed and wet some paper towels to clean myself up.

"Why are you with that nigga? He treats you like shit and I know he's puttin' his hands on you!" he yelled while he did the same.

"Why do you care? I'm not your problem to be worried about," I spat.

"Shayla, I have thought about you every day and night since the last time I saw you. Do you know how devastated I was when I woke up and you were gone? No number, no email, nothing. I couldn't even find you on social media because I didn't know your last name."

"Why would I give you my number? We had a fun few days together but that's all it was," I told him.

"That's not all it was to me, Shayla. I fell in love with you that weekend. And I've been trying to get you out of my system for the past year and a half but it's not working. I'm not letting you go back to him."

"Darius, I can't just leave okay. Kurt and I have a life together and ---"

"A life? You call being afraid all day a life? You deserve so much more Shayla."

"I gotta go back. He's probably gonna come looking for me any second," I pulled my dress down, realizing I had now had no underwear to put on.

I pushed past Darius and damn near ran back to the table. We had gotten our food and Kurt had already started eating. That's probably the only reason he didn't come and drag me out of the bathroom.

"Took you long enough! The fuck were you doing?" Kurt said, mean mugging me.

"I'm sorry. Did your friend leave?" I asked.

"Naw, he had to take a phone call. But you don't need to be worried about that nigga. I can see the way he's lookin' at you. Don't get fucked up in here!" Kurt warned.

"Kurt, I'm not doing anything to make him look at me. Why do you always make everything my fault?"

Darius came back to the table before he answered. The look on Kurt's face let me know that I'm gonna pay later for questioning him.

"How's the food? Looks great!" Darius said, looking directly at me.

"It's good," Kurt answered.

"I'm sure what we have is much better than the salad you ordered for your lady. Shayla, would you like some of my steak?" Darius asked as he began to cut it in half.

"No, she's good with her salad," Kurt replied for me.

"I didn't ask you, I asked her," Darius grabbed the saucer that my salad dressing had been on and put a piece of his steak on it, then slid it back to me.

"Umm, thank you, Darius. But I'm good with my salad," I told him, making no eye contact.

"You don't like steak?" he asked.

"Uhh, no I do. I, uhh, just would prefer this salad right now. Trying to watch my weight," I answered, smiling nervously, still no eye contact.

"You're beautiful just the way you are. You don't need to change a thing," Darius complimented.

Suddenly, Kurt pushed his chair away from the table and snatched my hand up, pulling me out of my chair. It happened so fast that I couldn't brace myself in my heels. I ended up on the floor with the chair on top of me.

"Shayla, get the fuck up and let's go. You and this nigga eye-fuckin' and flirtin' with each other like I ain't sitting here," Kurt screamed in my face. *You see what I mean?*

All eyes in the restaurant are on us, as Darius came to my aid, attempting to help me to my feet. That pissed Kurt off even more.

"Nigga, I'm not gon' tell you again! Keep ya muthafuckin' hands off my girl," Kurt yelled as he pulled Darius away from me by his shoulder, causing him to let me go and I fell again. *This can't be happening!*

That must have been the last straw for Darius because he punched Kurt dead in his face and a fight ensued. I finally got my ass off the floor and out of the way because with my luck, I'd end up on the other end of a punch that isn't meant for me this time.

I could hear police sirens in the distance. Two random men were able to separate them fairly quickly, and keep them apart. Kurt came towards me, pulling the guy along, and shouted in my face.

"I can't take your ass nowhere! You fuck everything up! Call an Uber and take your ass home!"

The police came in and put them both in cuffs and took them away. Darius looked at me, with pleading eyes and mouthed, "I love you", before turning away.

I went back to our table to get my purse and noticed something white sticking out of it. It was a hotel key, wrapped in a napkin that had the name of a hotel and room number. Sticking it back in my purse, I left the restaurant.

****

The next morning, I woke up to the sun shining brightly in my face, feeling better than I had in a long time. The last year and a half of my life has been pure hell and I'm ready to change that. I looked down at the handsome face sleeping so peacefully next to me and leaned in, planting a kiss on his plump lips.

"Good morning beautiful." he said, pulling me on top of him.

"Good morning handsome. When did you get in?"

"A few hours ago. I know things got crazy at the restaurant and I'm sorry."

"Don't apologize. It wasn't your fault," I told him.

Darius hugged me tight and placed kisses all over my face. "I thought I'd never see you again. I hope you know, I'm never letting you go."

"Where do we go from here?" I asked cautiously. Being with Kurt for almost two years has me wary of promises that others make.

"I think fate has brought us back together. Were you with Kurt the first time we met?" I was still lying on top of him. He looked into my eyes as he spoke.

"No, I actually met him about a month later. If he and I were together, I wouldn't have slept with you," I answered, a bit offended.

"That's not why I asked. I wouldn't care if you were. You're not now and that's all that matters. I'm serious when I say that I'm not letting you go. I want you to leave with me. Move to Miami with me."

I rolled back onto the bed and sat up, facing him, Indian-style. I can't believe he just asked me to move to Miami with him. We had a great connection when we met a year and a half ago. I was on a girl's trip with two of my friends. They ended up hooking up with some guys and went ghost on me. I was lying out on the beach, soaking up the sun and Darius approached me. We talked for hours before we found ourselves getting a room. We didn't leave the room for two days and made love in more ways than I thought possible. We shared so much about ourselves with each other that weekend that I probably know more about Darius than I know about Kurt. *But could I move to Miami with him?*

"Darius, I don't know. I mean, now that I've left Kurt, I don't plan on going back to him. He'd probably beat me to death. But moving to Miami with you? I don't know if that's a good idea either."

He sat up and took my hands in his. "Why? Tell me why you can't come with me."

I thought about it briefly and didn't have any solid reasons as to why I couldn't go. I honestly would love to. But after being so dependent on Kurt, I refused to run right into the arms of another man and allow him control over my life again.

"I would love to move to Miami," I paused, "but not with you. Let me explain," I put my hand up when I saw him about to make a fuss. "After being with Kurt and allowing him to rule over every part of my life, I can't do that again. I need to have my own place, pay my own bills, my own car, all of that. I stayed with Kurt because he took everything away from me. I had to quit my job because I was too embarrassed to go to work with all the bruises. He crashed my car and never replaced it. He kept me from my friends and the little bit of family that I have. All I had was him. I'm not doing that again," I explained.

"Shayla, I'm so sorry baby. God I wish I had known you were going through all of this. If I see Kurt's bitch ass again, I might kill that nigga," he pulled me to him and hugged me so tight. "But Shayla, I'm not Kurt. Why make me suffer for his fuck ups?"

"That's not what I'm doing. I was once a woman that took care of myself. I have two degrees and I've had amazing jobs. I let Kurt take all of that, along with my self-esteem, dignity, and self-respect. I want it back Darius. I'm not saying we can't be together, I'm just saying that we can't live together. Not right away anyway."

Darius laid back on the bed and didn't say anything for a few moments. I could tell that me not wanting to live with him right away bothered him. He's going to have to just deal with it. I lost myself loving a man, albeit the wrong man, and I can't do that again.

"Okay that's fine. Will you let me help you get settled?" he asked.

"Of course! I don't know anyone or anything about Miami." He pulled me on top of him again. "I'll help you find a place and I have a few connections that I can give you for a job. Your degrees are in business, right? Finance and Accounting?" I can't believe he remembered that.

"Wow! I'm impressed that you remembered."

"Baby I remember everything you shared with me that weekend. You wanna know what I remember most?" he asked while he pulled at the hem of his t-shirt that I slept in last night. I'm naked underneath.

"What do you remember most?" I whispered.

"This pussy!" He pulled the shirt over my head and flipped me over so that he was on top of me.

"Darius!" I giggled.

"I (*kiss*) could (*kiss*) never (*kiss*) forget (*kiss*) you (*kiss*) or (*kiss*) this (*kiss*) pussy," he planted kisses on my cheeks, forehead, and neck between each word. "You don't know how many times I prayed to God that I'd find you again."

He lowered his face and pressed his lips to mine. Gently, he pried my mouth apart with his tongue and slid it inside. Our tongues collided and danced around each other's. He only had on boxers and I felt his member grow hard against me.

We kissed, not like two people that had a brief encounter a year and a half ago. We kissed like two people in love. The passion and urgency was so strong. He communicated his need for me in the way that he kissed me and I've never felt more desired in my life.

It was the same way in Miami. Our connection was undeniable but I wouldn't let myself believe that we could be more than a weekend hookup. I was sure that me sleeping with him so quickly took me right out of girlfriend potential.

Our lips disconnected and Darius stood to remove his boxers. "I need to taste you. Can I do that?"

I nodded. He grabbed both of my ankles and put them on his shoulders. He traced his tongue from my ankle down to my inner thigh, getting on his knees to reach his goal. With my legs now resting on his shoulders, he dove into my honeypot.

"Ahhh!" I called out as his tongue caressed my clit. It's been so long since I've had my pussy eaten that I forgot how amazing it could be. Kurt stopped doing this a long time ago.

Darius used his tongue in ways that I've only read about in romance novels. He added his fingers to the mix and almost took me over the edge. He was relentless with how he used his mouth to bring me pleasure. I lost it when he stiffened his tongue and pushed it into my hole while circling my g-spot with his thumb.

"Darius baby! I'm cummin'!" I warned. I barely had the words out before my cream covered his face.

He must have really been turned on because he gave me no time to recover before he adjusted my legs on his shoulders and pushed all ten inches inside of me.

"Damn baby!" he said as he got balls deep inside of me. "This pussy is mine forever Shay. Do you hear me?"

I could hear him but I couldn't talk. I nodded instead but that wasn't good enough for his ass.

"Say it baby! I wanna hear you tell me it's mine," he demanded, grinding his ass and pushing deeper than I thought possible.

"It's---yours baby. This---pussy---is yours!" I breathed out.

"You gon' marry me Shayla. You gon' be my wife, you hear me?"

This pussy must be real good. "Ummm hmmm," I replied. "I'm cummin' again Darius."

"Shit, hurry up and cum then so I can bust this nut," he gave me two more deep strokes and it was a wrap. My juices squirted in every direction.

Darius quickly pulled out and released somewhere. I can't even tell you where because I was delirious but it wasn't inside of me.

"Aww shit! I forgot my baby was a squirter," he teased.

"Come shower with me so we can go pack up your stuff," Darius pulled me up and into the bathroom.

"I don't want anything. I went and got everything of importance last night."

"What about your clothes? You don't want to take anything?" he asked.

"Nope! I want to start over, fresh, with no reminders of Kurt."

"Okay then. Round two in the shower!"

Kay Shanee

THE END

4 BEST FRIENDS

Reign

"I don't know what you see in her." I told my best friend, Kaden.

We are hanging out in the living room of our apartment, not paying any attention to whatever is playing on Netflix. I'm sitting on the couch and he's lying down next to me with his head in my lap, while I massage his scalp.

"You say that about all the girls I talk to Rei," he replied, looking up at me.

"Have I been wrong?"

"Naw, I guess not. But you barely give them a chance. You know if ya'll don't get along then I ain't fuckin' with them."

This is true! Kaden and I have been best friends since we were in diapers. That's twenty years! Our bond is tighter than tight. I can't help it if the girls he chooses to date aren't good enough for him. There's nobody good enough for him. *Except me! Wait! Where'd that come from?*

"Why don't any of your little girlfriends ever like me anyway? I'm never mean to them in their faces," I asked Kaden. "They stay giving me attitude."

"It's not that they don't like you. They don't like how close we are. Even though I tell them over and over that we're just best friends."

Most people don't understand the dynamics of Kaden's and I relationship. Our moms are best friends and were pregnant with us at the same time. Kaden is exactly one month older than me. Our dads were best friends as well, until my dad died when I was six, which left my mom a widow and raising me alone. Kaden's parents divorced when we were seven.

Our moms ended up moving in together to save money so that they could open up a string of beauty supply stores. We were already close but living together made us even closer. In all these years, nothing sexual has ever happened between us. I wouldn't say that he's like a brother but we've never crossed that line. *Although I wouldn't mind. Huh? I didn't mean that, did I?*

When it came time for us to choose a college, we chose the same one. The only time we've lived apart since we were seven years old is our freshman year when we had to live in the dorms. Sophomore year, we got a two bedroom apartment together and we are now juniors.

"So basically they're insecure," I surmised as I finished massaging his scalp and gently tapped him to get off my lap.

"I guess so," he replied. "You done already?" he asked, referring to his scalp but not moving from my lap.

"Yes! I've been rubbing your head for twenty minutes Kae."

"I know but it feels good. Just ten more minutes," he said as he got comfortable again.

"Oh my God, Kaden!" I huffed.

Just as I started to rub his head again, his phone rang with a FaceTime call from his current boo. I didn't think he was going to answer it but he surprised me and picked up.

"Wassup Avery?"

"Nothing. What are you up to?" she asked, cheesing into the screen.

Avery is a pretty girl but I don't like her for Kaden. *I don't like anybody for Kaden.* There is something about her that rubs me the wrong way. He's been messing around with her for about a month. She's lasted longer than most.

"Nothing. Watching Netflix with Reign while she massages my scalp," he said, nonchalantly.

That's why these girls be spazzing on him. *Why would he tell her that?* He's always upfront with anyone he dates about who I am to him. At first, they're cool with it but when they see us interact with each other, it becomes a problem.

"Massaging your scalp? Umm, do you think that's appropriate for her to be doing?" Avery questioned, agitated.

"Her and my momma are the only two women that I let touch my hair. So yup!" Kaden told her.

Kaden does not play about his hair. He had hair that most women envied. Soft, thick, jet black and just past his shoulders in length. He usually wears it in braids but took them out earlier today, to wash and condition so that I could braid it fresh.

"Really Kaden? So you're sitting between another woman's legs while she rubs your head. Wow!"

"I'm not between her legs, my head is in her lap. See," Kaden turned the phone towards me and I smiled and waved. Avery looked like she wanted to come through the phone and strangle me.

"Are ya'll serious right now? How would you feel if I was laid up in some nigga's lap?" Avery yelled into the phone.

"First of all, Reign ain't just some nigga and if that's what you wanna do, then do you. Let me call you back!" Kaden pressed the end button and tossed his phone to the side.

"I don't know why you answered. And why did you have to tell her all that Kae?" I laughed.

"Hell, she asked what I was doing and I told her. Simple as that," he sat up and turned his back to me so that I could put his hair in a ponytail. "You want me to order a pizza or are you cookin'?"

"I took some chicken breasts out and I was gonna make Chicken Fettuccine Alfredo. But if you want your hair braided tonight, you'd better order a pizza. I'll make that tomorrow."

"Aww man Rei, you know that's my favorite. Now you got my taste buds wanting that," he whined.

"I can make it, but I'm not doing your hair tonight then."

"You know I'm not going out without my hair done Rei. I gotta be somewhere early tomorrow," he gave me a serious look.

"Well you have a choice to make," I went to the bathroom to wash my hands. When I came out, I walked to the kitchen and stood with my arms folded, waiting for him to answer.

"Come on Rei," he walked towards me. "I don't wanna choose. Hook me up," he pulled me towards him and tickled me until I was bent over, laughing hysterically with tears running down my eyes.

"Stop!" I said between breaths.

"You gon' hook me up? I thought you loved me Rei," he continued to tickle me. "I'm not stopping until you say yes."

I tried to get away from him and found myself trapped against the counter.

"Kaden, stop!" I yelled, laughed and cried at the same damn time. "I can't breathe!"

He eased up on the tickling and I stood up, trying to catch my breath. He held on to my sides and our chests were touching.

"You gon' cook for me and do my hair tonight Reign Storm," he called me by my full name with his lips poked out, pouting.

"Nope! You know I hate when you call me that." *What is going on with me? Why is our closeness making me feel this way? The throbbing between my thighs is not normal.* I put my hand on his chest, pushing him away to put some space between us.

"Pleeeaaasseee!" he begged as he tickled my sides, pulling me close to him again.

"Kaaddeenn, let me go. Okay, okay, okay. I'll do it!" I agreed, under duress but still laughing.

"I knew you loved me!" he gave me a big kool-aid smile then leaned in to kiss my cheek. But I turned my face towards his and our mouths collided.

As soon as our lips made contact, it felt like home. Neither of us pulled away. In fact, it's the exact opposite. It's as if he'd been waiting his whole life for this moment. Kaden grabbed both sides of my face, pressing his mouth hard against mine and pushing his tongue into mine. My tongue willingly met his and fought for control but he refused to relinquish it. I gave up and allowed his tongue to invade my mouth.

His hands moved down the sides of my arms then to my waist. He pulled me closer to him and away from the counter, sliding his hands down further to my ass. In one swift move, he lifted me up and I wrapped my legs around his waist and locked my arms around his neck. Our lips never separated. Breathing should have been a problem right now, but we used each other's breath to sustain one another.

Kaden pulled me from the counter, walked us to my bedroom and we fell onto my bed. He began to grind his rock hard dick against my pussy when finally, our lips parted and Kaden looked down at me before standing and pulling his shirt over his head.

I took a moment to enjoy the view. My eyes started at his waistline. Kaden had the perfect V-cut that women love and his basketball shorts exposed just enough to make me imagine what he's working with.

Traveling upwards, my eyes paused briefly on his well-defined 8-pack. God has truly blessed him. I've always thought Kaden was fine. He reminds me of Omari Hardwick but with longer hair. But lately, my thoughts have been shifting. I've woken up, one too many times, from the most erotic dreams with him as the star and my panties soaked. Masturbating to thoughts of him has become a morning ritual. When I made it to his face, we stared into each other's eyes, saying nothing, until I broke the silence.

"What are we doing?" I gasped, trying to catch my breath.

"I don't know Rei, but it feels right and I don't want to stop."

"Then don't!" *Please don't stop!*

Kaden

I stood between her legs and looked down at her. Reign is beautiful. Her skin is the color of cinnamon and so smooth that it looks airbrushed. Her deep, dark brown eyes are enclosed in long lashes. Perfect pouty lips that I am happy as fuck that I was finally able to taste. She works out religiously so her body is perfectly toned with curves in the right places.

"Reign, I love you. I'm in love with you. I've always been," I confessed.

I've been waiting damn near my whole life for Reign realize that I'm in love with her. Neither of us have been successful in the dating game. I've never tried to be, but she had a serious boyfriend about two years ago. It was the most painful three months of my life. He was a cool dude but I couldn't stand seeing them together. I would do the dumbest shit to cause friction between them and they eventually broke up. Reign didn't even realize that I was sabotaging her relationship.

"Wha--what? You're in love with me?" she sat up and took ahold of my hands pulling me down to sit next to her on the bed.

"Is that so hard to believe?"

My heart is pounding so hard, I would swear it was coming out of my chest. If Reign doesn't feel the same way about me, or isn't willing to explore what we could be, I've probably ruined our friendship with my confession.

"Kaden, I---I'm in love with you too. I think I've been in denial for---"

I didn't need to hear anything else. I grabbed the back of her neck and brought her face to mine. When our lips met for the second time, it was like an explosion. Our tongues collided until they were able to dance around each other. We kissed as if it was the only thing we were meant to do in this world.

I moved my hand up her arm and found the strap to her tank top, pushing it off her shoulder, then did the same with the other strap. Reign isn't too fond of bras and I thank God she isn't wearing one right now. I tugged the tank top down and her breasts sprang out, as we lay back on the bed. Tearing my lips away from hers, my tongue made its way to her neck, staying there momentarily to inhale her vanilla scent. As one hand caressed one breast, my tongue massaged the other, then switching it up to give the other breast some tongue action.

"Shit Kae," Reign whispered, as she ran her fingers through my hair that she had pulled from the ponytail.

I continued to use my tongue to familiarizing myself with her body, making my way down to a pair of my basketball shorts that she'd stolen a while back. I stuck my hand in the waistband of the shorts and her panties and my dick jumped when I felt her freshly waxed pussy.

"Can I taste it Rei?" I said between kisses on her stomach.

Instead of answering me, she began to push her tank top the rest of the way down and slide out of her bottoms. I didn't hesitate to assist her. There is no other woman as beautiful as Reign is to me. She lay before me, naked and completely exposed, allowing me to take in every inch of her body. This moment, this vision of beauty, will be ingrained in my memory, forever.

"Kaden, what's wrong? Why'd you stop?" she asked.

"You're so beautiful, Rei. I just wanted to look at you for a minute."

I kneeled down on the floor and pulled Reign by her ankles to the edge of the bed. She willingly placed her legs on my shoulders. My hands found her hips and I held her in place as I ran my tongue up and down the inside of each thigh. Her body shivered as she moaned. I kissed the top of her pussy and licked my way to her clit.

"Ahh shit!" she let out, giving me just the courage that I need to keep going since I'd never done this before.

My tongue circled around her clit and traveled slowly between her folds. Reign tastes like sweet, vanilla, pineapple, goodness. The wetter she got, the more I licked, the louder her moans became.

"Oh my God Kae, this feelsss---"

I took her bud between my lips and French kissed it like it was her mouth, then stuck my finger inside of her moist center. That sent her over the edge and she screamed my name.

"Kaden----oh my---shit---Kaaadeen," she screamed as she released her sweet nectar on face. That didn't stop me from lapping up every ounce of her juices until she began to scoot away from me.

"Wait Kae, stop. I can't take it," she gasped.

Reign managed to scoot to the middle of the bed. I stood and pushed down my shorts and boxers. My dick is hard as steel, pointing towards the ceiling. I could tell the exact moment that Reign saw it when her eyes got wide.

"What the fuck are you gonna do with that?"

I stroked my shit up and down, although it ain't necessary because I'm ready to bust right now.

I smirked. "You can handle it, Rei," I told her as I gently climbed on top of her.

"Umm, yeah, about that....," she paused, "Umm, I uhh, I've never, ummm, so yeah, I'm a virgin."

What? A virgin? Is she serious?

"Kaden, did you hear me?"

"Yes, baby, I heard you. So you and that busta ass nigga Leroy never---"

"His name is Lawrence and no. He just ate me out and that's it. Never went any further."

I sat next to her and rubbed my hand down my face, letting out a deep breath. It's rare that you will find a twenty-year-old woman that's still a virgin. I've always known that Reign was special. I know from experience that females these days will bust it wide open for damn near anybody, which is exactly why I couldn't fuck with them.

I've had plenty of females offer themselves to me but I couldn't bring myself to give that piece of me to just anyone. Don't get me wrong,

I've gotten hella head from numerous women. But I never reciprocated and never blessed them with the dick. I'm not like most niggas. Sex is too personal for me and I refuse to engage with anyone that I don't feel a connection. I've been waiting for Reign and it seems as if she's been waiting for me as well.

"I guess we'll have our first experience together," I leaned in to kissed her but she leaned back, putting her hand on my chest.

"What are you talking about? Are you----Kaden, you're a virgin?" she asked, baffled at my admission.

I didn't answer her. Instead, I leaned in again, this time she allowed our lips to mesh as we fell back onto the bed.

I maneuvered my body on top of hers, kissing her passionately. I've never been a kisser. A peck on the cheek, very rarely a peck on the lips, is the most a female has ever gotten from me. Women are too scandalous and I don't trust where their mouths have been. Just as easily as I convinced them to suck me off, some other nigga has probably done the same. The stirring in my stomach, every time our lips connected and our tongues intertwined, is a feeling that I don't think I'll ever get enough of. Reign is everything.

She opened her legs, allowing me to settle in between them, with my dick resting between the folds of her pussy. We grinded against each other and my dick slid up and down her slickness. The friction between us became so intense that Reign had another powerful orgasm.

"Damn Kae! What are you doing to me?" she said, breathlessly.

"Nothin' yet!" I expressed. "You ready?"

I could see the nervousness in her eyes but she nodded her head. I placed the tip of my dick at her entrance and had to bite my bottom lip because just that little bit had me ready to shoot up the club. I continued to press my way in and felt Reign's body tense.

"Relax baby," I whispered into her neck. "Relax."

She took a few deep breaths, releasing some tension. I'm only about a quarter of the way in. She's so damn tight that I'm beginning to wonder if my dick is too big.

"Just do it Kae! Just push it in," Reign demanded, squeezing my biceps.

"I don't want to hurt you Rei."

"It's gonna hurt either way. Just do it!" she repeated.

Against my better judgement, I did what she asked and in one swift movement, I was in heaven. However, from the sound that Reign made, she definitely was not.

"Owww shit Kaden!" she hollered.

"It's in now Rei," I told her, looking into her eyes.

"Now what?"

"Now we make love."

Reign

It's been two months since Kaden and I made it official. So far, I love having my best friend as my man. Nothing about our relationship has changed except for the fact that we make love, quite frequently I might add. It seems we can't get enough of each other. He's always been my protector and confidante, putting me first in every way. He's been treating me like a princess our whole lives, now he treats me like his queen.

However, we have yet to tell our parents about us being a couple. Kaden wanted to tell them from the jump. After the first time we made love, he was on the phone with his mom about tell it all until I stopped him. He didn't understand why I want to wait. I'm just nervous that they might not think us being together is a good idea. The school year has ended and we are going home for a couple of weeks before summer classes start. I can't avoid telling my family any longer so the plan is to tell them while we are home.

Some of our friends were surprised and others have always thought that there was something going on between us. It bothers me that people don't believe that we were truly just best friends and think we've been fucking on the low all this time. I guess it doesn't matter now because I can't deny my love for Kaden if I tried. And it's not just the best friend love that we've shared for all of these years. It's the kind of love that makes me smile at the thought of him, makes me excited to see him or to hear his voice. The kind of love that sends shivers down my spine with a simple touch and makes my panties wet with just a simple kiss on the lips. I love that man with my whole heart.

"Baby what are you over there daydreaming and smiling about?" Kaden asked from the other side of the bed.

"Huh? Oh nothing really?" I blushed.

"Oh it's something. You better had been thinking about me the way you were cheesing," he rolled over and kissed my cheek before getting out of bed.

"Actually it was. I was thinking about how great the past two months have been and how much I love you."

Kaden walked his naked ass back over to the bed and kneeled beside it. "You love me Rei?"

"Why do you sound so surprised? I've always loved you."

"Naw baby, that ain't what I'm talking about. Do you *love* love me?" he repeated.

"Yes Kaden, I *love* love you. Like you are my man. Like you got that good dick and that bomb head too!" I pushed him away and laughed.

"Oh so you just love this dick!" He stood up and began stroking himself.

"Hell yeah I love that dick. But I love the man it's attached to, too," I confessed.

"Well I love you too. Now come take a shower with me so I can give you this dick and show you how much," he pulled me out of bed and into the bathroom. We went two rounds in the shower and were late getting on the road to go home.

Kaden

We finally got on the road to head home a few hours behind schedule but that pussy was worth it. We wouldn't be this late but Reign had to take a nap because I wore her little ass out in the shower.

I'm excited to see my family and just chill for a couple of weeks. When we get back to school we have summer classes and then the start of our senior year. I'm anxious to finish out this last year of undergrad and start my life with Reign as my lady.

For some reason, she's nervous about telling our parents about us being in a relationship. Little does she know, they already know. I confided in my mom some time ago about my feelings for Reign. She told me to be patient and not force a relationship with her and allow it to naturally take place. I'm so glad I took her advice. Since our moms are best friends, of course my mom told Reign's mom. They both approve of us being together so I don't know why Reign thinks that this is gonna cause an issue.

"Kae, what do you think our moms and the rest of the family is going to say about us being a couple?" Reign's question pulled me out of my thoughts.

"It doesn't really matter baby. We're together whether they approve or not."

"I know but I don't---," She began before I interrupted.

"Listen Reign, I don't want you to worry about how they are going to react. Most of them probably thought we were fucking already anyway. They can accept it or they can get the fuck on," I reached over and rubbed her thigh. "Stop stressing baby," I told her.

"Okay. I'm sure it'll be fine. Do you want to tell them right away? You know everyone is going to be at the house when we get there," she asked.

"Why wait?"

****

A couple of hours later, we turned on our block and several cars lined the street. Whenever we came home to visit, our moms threw a party and invited all of our family and friends. Although this particular gathering is special, it's pretty much the norm.

"Looks like everyone is here," Reign observed.

"Well, we are kinda late," she looked at me and I winked which made her blush.

"Whatever! It's your fault," she tapped me on the shoulder.

"I'll take the blame since I did wear you out," I leaned over the console to give her a kiss. Our lips connected and what I only meant to be a peck turned into more. I pulled back after about a minute because my dick was about to push through my jeans.

"You want me to fuck you in this car, Reign?" I asked when we disconnected.

"Not right now but maybe later, you know they are not about to let us sleep in the same room," she said landing one more peck on my lips.

"Shit if they ain't. We grown as hell," I replied, irritated because she's probably right.

"Yeah, okay," she smirked.

We finally got out and left our luggage in the car since we had to park down the street from the house. I grabbed Reign's hand and pulled her close to me and noticed her resistance.

"Kaden, we can't walk in there holding hands. Let's at least tell them first," she pulled away from me.

"Man, we need to tell them asap because you know I can't be around you and not touch you. You trippin' Rei."

I'm glad this "secrecy" shit is almost over. We were glued by the hip before we became a couple and now she wants us to act like strangers. She's crazy as hell for that.

We made it to the house and went in through the front door. The house was empty but we could hear music and people talking in the backyard.

"Aye baby, let me go use the bathroom real quick," I went down the hall and into the bathroom, which I really didn't need to use. I sent my mom a text letting her know we were here. I flushed the toilet and ran some water before I exited the bathroom and found Reign in the kitchen looking in the pots.

"What are you looking for greedy?" I snuck up behind her, wrapped my arms around her waist and planted a kiss on her neck.

"I'm hungry. I wanna see what they cooked."

"Well let's go out back. I'm sure they've already started eating, you know, since we're late," I teased her again.

"Shut up!"

We lived in a nice sized house with a huge backyard. Hopefully our moms have everything set up like I asked and this goes off without a hitch. I let Reign walk out onto the deck area first. She wouldn't be able to see anything with how the tent was set up.

"Geez, our moms went all out for us this time. Are we celebrating something else?" Reign questioned.

I didn't respond as we continued across the deck and down the stairs to the yard. There was some family around the outside of the tent. Almost everyone was eating but several people stopped and greeted us with hugs. I didn't want to be rude but I need to make it to the tent.

"Let's go find our moms," I pulled Reign along.

We made it to the tent without anyone else stopping us. Most of the people here knew what was up so they followed behind us. Our moms greeted us as soon as we made it to the entrance of the tent.

"Hey babies! I'm glad ya'll finally made it so we can really get this party started," Reign's mom, Sharon, said as she gave us both hugs and kisses.

"You two look cute. I'm so happy you're home," my mom, Christine, said and gave us hugs and kisses as well.

Reign and I were both wearing white jeans with red shirts. I had on red 11's and she had on red Converse. We've coordinated outfits a few times since we've been a couple but today it was hard to convince her because she didn't want anyone to think we were together before we let the cat out of the bag.

"Reign, baby, I have a surprise for you. I need to put this blindfold on first," Sharon said.

"What? A surprise? For what?" Reign asked, confused.

"Just turned around so I can put this on. Nosy behind," Sharon fussed.

Reign turned around and looked at me, questioning me with her eyes. I shrugged my shoulders as if I had no idea what was happening. She begrudgingly allowed her mom to put the blindfold on. Once that was done, Sharon led her into the tent.

When we walked in, I was taken aback. I'm not even into this kind of stuff and I'm impressed. Our moms outdid themselves, decorating everything in red and white, which is both Reign and my favorite color. A small stage, more like a riser, is set up in front where the DJ was located. Sharon led Reign up there and I followed. Once Reign was in place, I took my position in front of her.

"Can we have everyone's attention?" the DJ said on the mic a few times to get everyone to settle down. Then gave the mic to Sharon.

"The guests of honor are here and as you all know, we have something special planned," Sharon informed the guests.

Reign stood there, still blindfolded, moving her head in each direction, as if she could see. I took the mic from Sharon and got on one knee. I gave my mom the signal to take the blindfold off of Reign.

She looked around and took in the decorations and the number of people before her eyes landed on me, kneeling in front of her.

"Oh my God!" she gasped and covered her mouth. Her eyes immediately began to water.

I took her hand in mine before saying, "Reign, you are my best friend. You've had my heart since the moment that I knew that I had one and I've loved you for even longer. I couldn't imagine my life without you in it and I've been waiting for the time to come for me to make you mine forever. Will you marry me?"

Reign didn't give me a chance to put the mic down and get the ring box from my pocket. She got down on her knees with me and pulled me into a hug, leaving kisses all over my face before she screamed.

"Yes, yes, yes, I will marry you!" she cried. "Oh my God Kaden. I love you so much. I can't wait to be your wife." The crowd ooohhed, aaahhed, clapped, and cheered when she accepted my proposal.

I stood and pulled her up with me. "Don't you want your ring first Rei?" I reached behind me to get it out of my back pocket. The room became relatively quiet again as the guests focused on the ring box.

I opened the box to expose a one carat, princess cut diamond ring. It may not be much to some but it almost wiped out my entire savings.

"I love it!" Reign cried as I put it on her finger.

"I love you! Welcome to our engagement party," I told her before I kissed her as if we were the only ones in the room.

"Congratulations!" the crowd sang as we kissed.

I'm grateful that everything went as planned. Soon I'll be marrying my best friend and the love of my life.

THE END

5 TRAPPED

Simone

Club Onyx was live tonight. My girls, Livvy, Renea, Autumn, and I, decided to hit the club, in celebration of Livvy's promotion at work, and Renea finishing up her Master's degree. We danced the night away in our little black dresses and four-inch heels. Now it's time for some grub.

"What ya'll feel like eating?" I asked.

"Breakfast!" they all said simultaneously.

I laughed as I slid into the back seat of Autumn's car. She's the designated driver for tonight.

"That's why ya'll my besties. I could definitely go for some breakfast food. Let's go to Waffle House," I suggested.

"I would rather have pancakes or French toast. Let's do Denny's," Renea said.

"That's cool too." I replied.

We rode in silence for the fifteen minute drive to the nearest Denny's. All except Autumn were tipsy. She parked the car and we all took our time getting out. As hungry as I am, my bed sounded just as inviting as these pancakes I'm about to smash.

As we walked into the restaurant, my eye caught a group of guys sitting in the back corner. *Shit!* Just my luck that Omari and his boys are here. The hostess took us to our seats, which happened to be in the same section as Omari's group. *Dammit!* But I'm not gonna cause a scene and ask to be moved.

"Hey guys!" Autumn spoke to the group first, then we all followed suit.

"Wassup ladies!"

"How ya'll doing tonight?"

"Damn, ya'll looking good as hell!"

All of the guys spoke except for Omari. He was too busy staring at me to say anything.

"Where ya'll coming from?" Steven asked. I don't think he was talking to anyone in particular but his gaze never left Autumn. He's had a thing for her for a while but he has too much baby mama drama so she won't give him the time of day.

"Club Onyx," Autumn replied. "What about you guys?"

"Shit, nowhere. We were just chillin' at my crib, playing the game and having a few drinks. Then we got hungry and ended up here," Steven told her.

Omari gazed remained focus on me and he had yet to speak until he finally said, "Simone, let me talk to you for a minute." I knew Omari wouldn't let this moment pass.

"I'll be right back. Order me the Double Berry Banana Pancake Breakfast and a water," I slid out of the booth and followed Omari.

As soon as we were outside, he pulled me to him and kissed me. I didn't pull away because kissing Omari is one of my favorite things to do. His lips feel like satin rubbing against mine as he pushes his tongue into my mouth. I received it willingly, releasing a moan as his hands found their way to my ass. I didn't want him to pull away and was disappointed when he did. He kept me close to his body and his hand remained on my ass.

"What do you need to talk to me about?" I said, breathlessly.

"You didn't tell me you were going out tonight and why are you wearing this little bitty ass dress?" he complained. Just like that, he ruined the whole mood.

"Omari, why do we have to keep going over this? YOU are not my man," I pushed away from him, forcing him to release his hold on my ass.

"Yeah yeah! You keep saying that shit but I'm not feeling it. We do everything that couples do and we only do those things with each other. I don't see why we can't make this official," he ranted.

"Because I don't want to be in a committed relationship right now," I answered him, although he knew the answer because we've had this conversation a hundred times.

"Right now? It's been two years Simone. We've been fucking for two years," he repeated, "and you're still not ready to commit. What am I supposed to do? I've been real patient. I'm almost thirty years old and ready to get married and start a family. I want to do that with you," he confessed.

I knew all of this. We go through this every three months or so. I'm happy with where we are in our relationship. He's the only one I'm having sex with and he says I'm the only one he's having sex with. We hang out at each other's homes, we go out to dinner and movies, we've even met the important people each other's lives. As he said, we do everything that couples do. But I don't want to be in a committed relationship and Omari is going to have to accept it.

"Baby, I know how you feel and what you want. When I'm ready to commit, you will be who I commit to. I just ---"

"You better hope I'm still around," he interrupted before he yanked the restaurant door open and stormed inside.

I let him get to his table before I went inside. Thankfully, our food had arrived and the girls were already eating. My appetite decreased substantially after my conversation with Omari. But I ate some of my food and took the rest to go.

Omari didn't look my way or acknowledge me again. He didn't even say goodbye and I must say, that kind of hurt my feelings. As soon as we got in the car, the girls threw a ton of questions my way.

"What happened?"

"What did he say?"

"Did you piss him off?"

"Why do you keep playing with his emotions?" they went on and on but I didn't have much to say. They knew the status of Omari and my relationship and they knew why I didn't want to commit.

"Omari knew what it was when we started this thing. I don't know why he's always trippin'." I finally replied.

"Maybe because it's been two years and he thought you'd get with the program by now." Renea spoke up.

"We didn't put a time limit on our situation. It's not my fault that he wants to switch shit up. I'm not about to talk about this with ya'll because you're always on his side. Autumn drop me off first." They got the picture and ended the conversation.

We rode to my house in silence. "Text me when you guys get in. Love you." I told them as I got out of the car. Autumn waited until I entered my home and locked up before she pulled off.

I took my shoes off before I turned the alarm on and walked upstairs to my bedroom. Once inside, I pulled my dress over my head and put it in my hamper. I toyed with the idea of skipping the shower but quickly decided against it. On my way to the bathroom, I heard my text message notification, so I picked up my phone on the way to turn on the shower.

O: You home yet

Me: Yup

O: Come open the screen door

WTF! What is he doing here? He's the last person I would think would be at my door right now with the way that he behaved at Denny's. I turned the shower off and went downstairs to open the door. He has a key but I locked the screen door since I wasn't expecting him.

I looked out of the window and saw Omari standing there. I turned off the alarm, unlocked and opened the door, standing off to the side since I didn't bother to put my robe on and I was still in my panties and bra.

"Really Simone?" he said when he saw me before turning to close and lock the door.

"What? It's three a.m. and I was about to get in the shower. What are you doing here anyway?"

"I wanted to see you. We need to talk."

"You know what, we've talked enough for the night and it didn't end well. You can talk to yourself. I'm going to shower," I turn around and went upstairs, leaving Omari downstairs. I know what he wants to talk about and I'm tired of the conversation. I especially don't want to talk about it at three a.m.

I stood in the shower, allowing the water to run down my body, including my head. *Why can't Omari just accept that a relationship is not what I want?* I was lost in my thoughts when I felt a gust of cold air as the shower door opened. I didn't turn around because, of course, it was Omari.

I heard the shower door close and felt the heat radiating from his body. He grabbed me by the waist and pulled my back to his chest. When his lips connected to my neck, any resistance I planned to give went straight out of the window. I have such a weakness for this man. When my mind told me that I needed to end things with him, so that he could move on and find someone to build a life with, my body told me that he was mine and always would be.

I leaned my head back to rest on his chest, allowing him to access more of my neck. Unwillingly, a moan escaped my lips. His hand slid down the front of body and found my bare mound. As usual, I'm already wet for him and he slipped two of his fingers inside of me.

"Sssss," I breathed as his fingers dipped in and out.

He gripped my wet hair and pulled my head back so that he could access my mouth with his. Our tongues collided before finding a rhythm. Omari knew just what to do to bring me to a climax quick. His fingers jetted in and out of me with just the right amount of speed and pressure.

"Ahhh shit!" I exclaimed into his mouth.

Without giving me time to recover, Omari flung me around and against the cold shower wall. I looked up at him and his eyes were filled with a look of...no it couldn't be. I shook my head and dismissed those thoughts. Surely Omari is not in love with me.

He grabbed me by the hips, lifting me enough to push his full length inside of me, as I wrapped my legs around his waist. My breath hitched, as it always does upon his entrance.

"Omari, we need a condom," I whispered but really couldn't see myself allowing him to leave me to get one. It felt too good.

He began to roll his hips, pushing himself even deeper. "Omari, you forgot a cond---," I began.

He thrust himself upward, taking away my ability to think and speak. Omari has the kind of dick that will make you slap your grandmother for smiling at him. *But it's not good enough to make you commit to him.* My thoughts are all over the place as he pumped in and out without an ounce of gentleness. It hurt so good that all I could do is scream as my climax began to build.

"Shit baby, don't stop! Don't you fuckin' stop Omari! I'm about to cum," I screamed. I used my thighs to squeeze his hips and the heels of my feet to push him deeper, if that was even possible.

"Oh damn baby! You feel so good. I'm cumin' now. Right now I'm cumin. Ahhh, shit Omari baby!"

As I released my juices all over his dick, I could feel him pulsing inside of me. I was so gone that it took me several seconds to realize that this nigga didn't pull out.

"Oh my God Omari! You didn't pull out!" I yelled as I dropped my legs from around his waist and I tried to push him away. He was still recovering from busting that nut so his weight was heavy on me, still pressed against the wall.

I hit his shoulder a couple of times and pushed him again. He finally began to budge. When he looked at me, he had a sly smirk on his face.

"What the fuck Omari? Why didn't you pull out?" I yelled at him again.

"What's the big deal Simone? Aren't you on the pill?" he asked as he stepped back, grabbed his soap and towel, and began to wash up like he didn't just let off a load of semen inside of me. *This nigga!*

"Really O? First of all, you know we always use condoms. Secondly, you know I haven't been on the pill for over a year. Fuck Omari? What if I get pregnant?"

He was irritating the hell out of me with his nonchalant attitude. He finished washing and rinsing and stepped out of the shower, without answering my question and leaving me standing there with the water turning cold. I quickly washed up and found him in my bed, under the covers.

"So you're gonna ignore me?" I threw my towel at him.

"Just take a morning after pill since you act like having my baby would be the end of the world," he turned over and pulled the covers up to his neck.

"Don't do that Omari. This is not about having YOUR baby? I don't want to have anybody's baby. And you know I'm not gonna take no damn Plan B. You know how I feel about that. I can't believe you didn't use a condom. I swear to God, if I'm pregnant, I'm gonna---"

Omari sat up quickly in the bed and yelled, "You're gonna do what Simone?" he paused briefly, waiting for me to answer. When I didn't, he continued, "You know what. Fuck this shit. I can't do this anymore. I love you too fuckin' much to continue whatever this is that we got going on."

He threw the comforter back and went to one of the drawers that he had in my room. He grabbed some clothes and quickly got dressed. I watched him as my vision became blurry as my tears pooled in my eyes.

"I guess I'll see you around. I'm out!" He snatched his wallet and keys from the dresser and left.

I wanted to run after him. There was something final about what he said and the tone of his voice. I wanted to beg him not to leave but I was frozen in place. I heard him turn on the alarm and leave. He said that he loved me too much. *Could it have been love that I saw in his eyes?* But love wasn't a part of our plan. *We weren't supposed to fall in love O?*

I repeatedly told myself that Omari was just upset and things will be back to normal in a couple of days then crawled into bed and cried myself to sleep.

*******2 Months Later*******

Things were not back to normal in a couple of days. It's been two months and Omari is not answering my calls nor is he replying to voicemails and texts. I tried calling him from other phone numbers and still couldn't reach him. I even went by his house several times and he had gotten his locks changed so I couldn't use my key. His mom refuses to be in the middle of our shit because in her eye, we should already be married and given her at least one grandchild by now. Those were her exact words. I'm really close to making a damn fool of myself and going to his job.

I miss Omari something terrible. I find myself stalking his social media pages and looking at old pics and videos of us that I had saved in my phone. He's never gone this long without communicating with me in some way. I finally had to stop denying, probably in about week three of no contact with Omari, that I love him. I don't just love him, I'm in love with him. But now he won't even talk to me so that I can tell him.

From the moment that I realized that Omari could very likely be done fucking with me, I've been sick. The fear of him moving on had me literally vomiting. I've been in a state of depression for a month. My girls finally forced their way into my house after I avoided them for two whole months.

"Oh my God Simone! What is your problem?" Renea asked.

I hadn't told them anything about what went down with Omari. I simply avoided them by telling them that I was swamped at work, which happens sometimes, and they didn't press the issue.

"Omari hates me," I whined then began bawling.

"What?" Livvy said, confused. "Why would he hate you?"

"Yeah, I mean, I know he's tired of you playing games but that man loves your dirty draws. I don't think it's possible for him to hate you," Autumn chimed in.

"But he does! He left and I haven't seen or talked to him in two months," I cried.

"Two months!" they said at the same time.

"He won't answer his phone or reply to my texts. He changed his locks. He hates me," I sobbed.

"Damn girl, you must have rally fucked up!" Renea exclaimed.

"Renea, stop being so insensitive. Geez!" Autumn said, hitting Renea on the shoulder.

"My bad! Let's sit down so you can tell us what the hell happened," Renea suggested, softening her tone.

We walked into my den and we all found a seat. I've lived that night over and over in my head a hundred times and I was not looking forward to doing it again. But I told my girls what happened and their reaction was not what I expected. Well, maybe it was because they've been #TeamOmari for a minute.

"Simone, you said you saw love in his eyes and he later said that he loved you. What don't you understand?" Renea grilled me.

"If you don't want to be with him. Let him go. That man deserves to be with someone that wants to be with him just as much as he wants to be with them. You don't want to give that to him so let him go!" That was

Livvy speaking. She generally wasn't as harsh as Renea but she's not holding back now.

"I don't want him to be with anyone else. I want to be with him. Okay? I realized in the last two months that I love him too. But he won't talk to me," I continued crying and they offered me no sympathy.

"Are you pregnant?" Autumn asked.

"What? I don't know. I haven't thought about it. I don't think so," I replied.

"Well let's find out," Autumn dug in her purse and pulled out a pregnancy test. We all stared at her in disbelief.

"Hoe, why do you have a pregnancy test in your purse?" Renea asked.

"Because I needed to restock and I keep forgetting to take them out of my purse. I have a few other brands in here as well," Autumn replied as if it was normal to have pregnancy tests in your purse.

"You know what, I'm done with your ass," Renea shook her head as she replied.

"What? Ya'll should be glad I have them. Now we don't have to go to the store," Autumn threw a box to me. "Go pee on that stick," she demanded.

I slowly rose from the couch and walk to my guest bathroom. I prayed as I went through the process of taking the test. "God please let this be negative. Omari wants nothing to do with me and I don't want to raise our baby alone."

"Hurry up!" I heard Livvy say.

"I'm done. I'm just waiting for it to---oh God. Oh nooooo!" I cried and they barged into the bathroom, causing me to drop the stick on the floor.

Autumn tore off a piece of tissue and picked up the stick. "Oh my God! We're having a baby!" she screamed excitedly.

The three of them pulled me into a group hug while singing, "we're having a baby", over and over. *How can they be so excited when I'm in shock?*

"You guys, this isn't good. Omari hates me and he probably already has someone else," I began bawling again. They walked me out of the bathroom, to the den, and sat around me on the couch.

"Simone, sweetie, I'm sure when you tell him, he will be ecstatic. He probably did the shit on purpose to trap your non-committing ass," Renea said. I'm sure she thought that she was comforting me but she definitely was not.

"Renea!" Livvy yelled. "Why would you say something like that? What guy traps a woman anyway?"

"Umm, guys that are so in love with a woman who doesn't seem to feel the same way," Renea continued.

"He wouldn't!" Autumn gasped.

"He would and he did!" Renea said, very sure of her assumption.

"I need ya'll to go. I want to be alone. I need to process this shit," I spoke.

"Well damn! Just use a bitch pregnancy test and kick her out," Autumn joked.

"No seriously. I need to think and I can't do that with ya'll all up in my ear talking crazy," I got up and walked to the door, letting them know I'm serious. "Thank you for coming to check on me, I'll call ya'll tomorrow."

"Okay we leaving damn!" Livvy said. They all grabbed their purses and left, promising to break my door down if I don't call them tomorrow.

Omari

I can honestly say that I've been miserable. So miserable that I've made myself sick. After forcing myself to stay away from Simone for two months, I began to feel my resolve wearing thin. I love her and I can't see my life without her. Her issues with commitment are something that I don't understand. I assume that she had her heart broken at some point and she was making me suffer for some other nigga's fucked up ways. I had no idea that agreeing to a "friends with benefits" relationship with her would turn into me catching feelings and her not wanting to commit after two years. As much as she denies it, I know Simone feels the same way about me as I do about her.

When I decided to end things with her, I had to see her one more time. I went to her house after leaving Denny's, with the intention of spending one last night with her, telling her I loved her, something I've wanted to tell her but never had the nerve to, and giving her one more chance to give a title to our relationship.

I replayed that night in my head. When I slid up in her raw, my mind went to another place. Simone's pussy is made for me and me alone. The way her walls hugged my dick had me gone. In the two years that we've been fucking, I've never slipped up and not used a condom. I didn't slip up this time. I had no intentions on wrapping up but I was going to pull out.

As my dick found it's home inside of her, I imagined my future with her. I saw her as my wife and the mother of my children. With each thrust, I lost all logic and reasoning. I began to think that if she gets pregnant, she will commit. I ignored her pleas about getting a condom and pushed myself deeper inside of her. That caused her to change her tune and demanding that I not stop. I felt my nut rising and the thought of pulling out was long gone. Within seconds, we were both in orgasmic heaven but shortly after, she came to her senses.

My cell phone ringing took me out of my thoughts from that night. I answered it without looking to see who it was.

"Hello."

"Omari, please don't hang up!" Simone pleaded. It sounded like she'd been crying.

"Simone? Are you okay?" I asked.

"No, yes, I --- I need to see you," she stammered.

"Simone, I don't think that's a good idea. I can't ---," I began.

"Omari, please. We need to talk," she begged again.

"Fine, I'll be over shortly."

"I'm outside," she stated quickly, "please open the door."

As soon as she spoke those words, I began to walk towards my door. *What the hell?* I reached the front door and opened it quickly. We both still had the phone up to our ears when our eyes connected. I had to restrain from grabbing her and pulling her into a hug and kissing her plump lips. Damn I've missed her so much.

"How long have you been here?" I asked as I removed the phone from the side of my face and stepped to the side so that Simone could come in. She stepped in but didn't answer my question. I closed the door and turned to face her. We were still in the entryway of my house.

"You wanted to talk?" I stood with my arms folded across my chest. That's the only way I could keep my hands to myself.

"Can we go sit?" she timidly asked.

I nodded my head and we went to my living room. She sat on the couch and I sat across from her, in my recliner.

"I'm listening," I said coldly. It wasn't my intent to be so cold because Lord knows I wanted to feel her in my arms. But my words came out that way.

She let out a long breath before she began. "My mother was, probably still is, a habitual cheater. She cheated on my dad for their entire relationship. When my mom would be out all night, sometimes not coming home for days, my dad would go off on angry rants. I look a lot like my mom so when he saw me, I reminded him so much of her, he would take out all of his anger for her, on me. He'd say that I was a whore, just like my mother. That no man would ever commit to me because I'm just like my mother. He even said that he wasn't sure that I was his daughter until he got a DNA test," she paused briefly as tears slid down her face. I wanted to go to her and comfort her but I wanted her to say what she had to say, with no interruptions.

"The older I got, the more I started to believe that my dad was right. So I decided that I never wanted to be in a committed relationship because I never wanted to put a man through what my mom put my dad through. She ruined him to the point that he couldn't love his own daughter. Now he's in prison for first degree murder and attempted murder. He killed one of my mother's lovers and tried to kill her but she survived. I cut all ties with both of them."

"Shit!" was all I could manage to say. This definitely explained her fear of commitment. I tried to find the words to say but nothing, and I do mean nothing, came to mind.

"I'm sorry O. I'm sorry for stringing you along for all this time. I'm sorry for making you feel like you aren't worthy of commitment because you are. I'm sorry that I dismissed your feelings. If you never want to talk to me after I leave here, I won't ever bother you again. I just want you to know that---that I love you! I'm in love with you. Can you please give me another chance?" her tears were nonstop at this point.

She got up and came to me, kneeling in front of me, positioning herself between my legs.

"How do you know that you're in love with me?" I asked as I wiped her tears with my thumbs.

"I've missed you so much. I've been miserable without you. The aching in my heart hasn't stopped since you walked out, I've been sick, I can't ---"

I'd heard enough. I pulled her face to mine and silenced her with a kiss. These last two months I've felt like I was suffocating and when our lips touched, I finally felt like I could breathe again.

"Omari, I have something else I need to tell you," she said when she pulled away.

"I don't want to talk right now," I leaned in to regain my connection to her lips.

"But this is important. It really can't wait," she turned her head so that I kissed her cheek instead.

I haven't seen or been with her for two months. All I want is to be inside of her. This better be important.

"Okay. I'm listening," I conceded.

She stood and pulled my arm, indicating that she wanted me to stand up, and we both went to the couch to sit.

"I don't know how to say this," she started.

"Just say it baby."

"I um---I haven't had---well---," she stammered.

"Baby, what is it. You can tell me."

Instead of talking, she reached in her purse and handed me the plastic baggie that she took out of it. I looked at the white stick, not knowing what I was looking at for a moment. I turned it around and saw the words PREGNANT in an oval. I looked at Simone for clarification and she had a timid smile on her face.

"Are you? Is this? Noo, this can't be right," I said in disbelief.

"Are you upset?"

"Upset? No, no! Damn, we're having a baby?" I looked at the test again and I couldn't contain my happiness.

I wrapped my arms around her shoulders and planted kisses all over her face and neck.

"You gon' have my baby?" I asked between kisses.

"Do you want me to?" she questioned.

"Hell yeah!" I kissed her again. "You're gonna be my wife. That's not a question. I'm telling you that you will be my wife. Before this baby is born, we're getting married."

"Omari," she pushed back to look me in my eyes. "We don't have to get married just because I'm pregnant. Let's see how this relationship works out first."

"I don't want to marry you because you're pregnant. I want to marry you because I love you. Simone, listen. You are not your mother. Just because she gave birth to you and you look like her, doesn't mean you're going to turn out like her," I assured her as tears streamed down her face.

"I know but I don't want us to move too fast. Let's just ---"

"Too fast? In the past two years, have you been with anyone besides me?"

"No! What the fuck Omari? Why would you ask that?" she said angrily.

"Because, you need to realize that just because we didn't put a title on what we were, we were still in a committed relationship. You are not your mother Simone."

She didn't say anything. I got up and went to my bedroom to get something that I wanted to give her. I've been holding on to it for quite some time. When I returned, she looked up at me and gave me a weak, teary-eyed smile.

I sat on the couch next to her and took her hands. "Simone, my prayer every night for the past year and a half, ever since I realized that I was in love with you, has been that one day, you would feel the same way about me. I've felt for a long time that you did but I knew that you weren't acknowledging those feelings. But I never stopped praying. So you coming here today lets me know that my prayers have been answered."

I got down on one knee in front of her and pulled the ring out of my sweats. When she realized what was happening, her hand went to her mouth and more tears fell from her eyes.

"I need you to know that I don't want to marry you because you are carrying my seed. I've had this ring for eighteen months. I bought it when I knew that I was in love with you. I knew that my prayers would get answered. Simone, will you do me the honor of becoming my wife?"

Simone wrapped her arms around my neck while nodding. "I need to hear you say it baby. Will you marry a nigga?"

"Yes, baby. Yes, I'll marry you."

THE END

6 AGE AIN'T NOTHIN' BUT A NUMBER

I swear I don't want to go out tonight. But I promised my best friends, Candyce and Patryce, that I would. I haven't been out in a minute, since my boyfriend and I broke up. Hell, now that I think about it, it's been over six months. *Now that's just sad, Coco.* Just thinking about my ex made me want to crawl under my bed. But I knew that wouldn't be happening this time. Candyce and Patryce weren't having it, but I'm ready to let loose and have a little fun.

I checked myself out in the full length mirror, admiring the view. Don't get it twisted, I'm definitely a ten in the looks department. Most people find it hard to believe that I am thirty-nine years old. Deep, smooth, chocolate skin. Naturally curly hair that I've worn in an afro since before it was cool to do so. Physically fit because the gym is my boo. Standing at 5'7" but I looked taller because of my long, lean legs. Getting a man has never been an issue, keeping one is the problem. I haven't had many serious relationships, only three to be exact, in my adult life. Two of them ended right at the three month mark and this last one, lasted eight whole months. I thought Jason was the one but his ass had me fooled. *Why do I keep thinking about his ass?*

Thankfully, a text came through from Patryce saying that they were outside. I texted her back and quickly took a few full body selfies to post on my social media pages before grabbing my purse and locking up my condo. I rushed down the hallway with my face in my phone and as I rounded the corner, I ran into a hard body.

"Oh shit!" I gasped, as my phone and the contents of my little clutch purse spilled onto the floor. I kneeled down, very prim and proper like, because my ass is already damn near hanging out of my dress, to pick up my belongings. I didn't even look up to see who I had bumped into, but his voice did something to me.

"My bad sweetheart," I heard, right next to my ear. I looked in the direction of the deep, sexy voice and damn near passed out.

"Uhh, no, I should've been paying attention. It's my fault," I said in a whisper, as I slowly reached for my items on the floor, but totally missing them. I was so taken aback by the beautiful man whose face was mere inches away from mine, I completely lost all train of thought.

"Let me get this for you," he gently grabbed the clutch from me and began placing my belongings inside, as I stood and watched him, mesmerized.

"Thank you," I managed to get out when he stood and handed me my purse.

"Not a problem. I'm Malcolm," he reached out for a handshake.

"Coco. And again, I'm sorry. I was looking at my phone and...," I began before he interrupted.

"No worries, Coco," he took my hand and pulled it to his lips, kissing the back of it.

His lips were so soft, a little wet, and sent a tingle directly to my pussy. Normally, I would have been disgusted but I was too busy imagining those wet lips on my lower set of even wetter lips. I don't know how long we stood there, with my hand still in his, eyes locked, before my phone buzzed and took us out of our trance.

"Oh, I, uhh, it was nice meeting you, Malcolm. My friends are waiting for me," I finally got it together, pulled my hand from his grip, and attempted to continue my way to the elevator. If I stood there any longer, I'd be wrapping my legs around his waist.

"The pleasure was all mine beautiful," he smiled, a smile so beautiful that I probably should have been going back to my condo to change my underwear. But instead, I turned away from him and put an extra switch in my hips cause I knew he was watching.

As soon as I made it to the car, Candyce and Patryce immediately started fussing at me.

"What the hell took you so long Coco?" Patryce started.

"I thought I was gonna have to come grab your ass outta bed!" Candyce yelled.

"Whatever bitches! I ran into my future husband in the hallway and got a little distracted," I told them as I slid into the back seat.

"Future husband?" they both said.

"That's what I said! His name is Malcolm and he's fine as hell."

"Hold up," Patryce said as she turned the radio down and turned in her seat to face me. "You need to give more details than that."

"Nope! It's not that big of deal anyway. I was just kidding. I mean, I did bump into a fine ass dude named Malcolm but that was all it was," I told them. I didn't feel like going into details.

"Hmm. Well maybe you'll run into him again," Candyce said before she turned the volume back up on the radio.

We arrived at *Club Liquid* about fifteen minutes later. When I saw the line, I immediately began to regret agreeing to go out.

"Damn! That line is ridiculous so you know we're gonna have to park a mile away," I complained.

"Shut up with your complaining Coco! *Club Liquid* is always packed. You'd know that if you came out with us more often. It's been this way since it opened six months ago," Patryce explained.

"I can't believe you guys come here all the time. Please tell me you have some kind of VIP and don't stand in this line. This shit is ridiculous," I ranted on.

"The line moves fairly quickly. Ha! And look, I found a decent parking spot," Candyce squealed as she turned into the space.

"I hope your luck continues and we can get in this place before it closes!" I know I'm being a spoiled brat but this is half the reason I don't do clubs. Lounges, sure, but the club scene is overrated.

We all checked our makeup and exited the vehicle. The line did look like it was moving fairly quick, so I felt better about this but I still would leave right now if given the chance.

"Oh-My-God!" I heard Patryce say.

"What?" Candyce and I asked simultaneously.

"Look at that nigga right there!" She nodded her head in the direction of said nigga and we followed her gaze.

"Shit!" Candyce let out.

"I can't believe it," I said to myself more than them.

"What?" they asked.

"That's him. That's the guy I bumped into in the hallway of my building."

I told them.

"Damn! He is gorgeous. What did you say his name was? Malcolm?" Patryce asked.

I didn't reply because I couldn't take my eyes off of him. He must have felt me staring because he turned in my direction and our eyes connected. He smiled and my pussy pulsed.

"He's looking over here," Candyce whispered.

"He's walking this way," Patryce exclaimed quietly.

I stood speechless until he was standing in front of me. This man is beautiful. I know that's weird to say when describing a man but I can't think of another word. Dark chocolate skin, light brown eyes, perfectly aligned white teeth. A body for the gods! *Damn!*

"Coco, nice seeing you again so soon," Malcolm spoke first, reaching for my hand. I gladly gave it to him and allowed him to press his beautiful, full lips against the back of it for the second time tonight. Just as it did before, my pussy purred at his touch.

"Ahh, yeah. You too," I finally found my voice.

"Hello! I'm Patryce, this is my twin sister Candyce. We are Coco's best friends," Patryce stuck her hand out for him to shake. He continued to hold my hand and my attention. He didn't take his eyes away from mine.

"Nice to meet you ladies," he said without looking their way. "I'm sure you don't want to wait in this line. Would you be interested in coming in with me and my boys and joining us in our VIP section?"

"Uhh...," I started but Candyce answered for us.

"We sure would!"

I gave Candyce a look that said, *what are you doing,* as Malcolm pulled me to his side to walk next to him. We made our way to the entrance, with Candyce and Patryce right behind us, and Malcolm's group of friends behind them.

"Aye Malcolm, wassup?" the bouncer said to Malcolm as they dapped each other up.

"Nothin' much man. Came out to celebrate Jordan's birthday. Is the spot ready?" Malcolm conversed with the bouncer.

"Everything's ready. I'll holla at you later." The bouncer stepped back and unhooked the red velvet rope to let us through.

Malcolm held my hand as we entered the club. It was like the parting of the Red Sea as we walked through the crowd. Everyone moved out of the way to allow us, well him, to walk through.

We continued to the back part of the club and approached a set of stairs. Malcolm finally let my hand go and allowed me to walk ahead of him. *Probably looking at my ass.* When I got to the top, I was taken aback. I don't frequent VIP sections but none that I have ever been in was this dope. It was damn near a miniature club by itself.

"Wow!" I exclaimed as I paused at the top of the stairs, before continuing to a seating area.

"Damn, this is nice!" Patryce expressed with excitement.

"I'm glad you ladies like it. There are bartenders and a wait staff dedicated just to this area. The bar is over there, around that corner. Feel free to go and get yourselves some drinks. If you're hungry, you can place an order for food there as well. Or, once you are seated, the waitress can take your orders. Everything is on the house," Malcolm offered.

"That's wassup!" Candyce said, grabbing my and Patryce's hands and pulling us towards where Malcolm indicated the bar was located.

"Thank you," I said as Candyce pulled me along.

"Oh my God! You ain't lie when you said he was fine. It seems like he's paid too. If you don't hop on that niggas dick, I sure as hell will," Candyce spoke as we made our way to the bar.

"He is fine but the birthday boy is more my type. I wonder if he has a woman?" Patryce said, more to herself than to us.

They ordered some kind of fruity alcoholic drink and I just got a bottle of water.

"Coco, are you serious right now? Malcolm said that everything is on the house and you're getting a bottle of water?" Candyce questioned, looking at me sideways.

"I don't think I'm gonna drink tonight. It's been a minute and I need to keep my head together around this man. He's doing something to me and we've barely said ten words to each other," I told them.

"Shit, he's doing something to me too." Candyce said lowly.

See, Candyce is gon' make me whoop her ass. Even though we are "best friends", there has always been an unspoken competition between us. Well, at least on her end. She is always trying to one up me and it is very annoying at times. Usually I ignore her ass but I may have to say something tonight.

We got our drinks and went back to the main area of VIP. I spotted an open couch and walked in that direction. Before I was able to sit down, Malcolm gently grabbed my elbow to guide me to where he and his friends were sitting. Patryce and Candyce followed.

"You think I brought you up here for you to sit and gossip with your girls?" Malcolm whispered in my ear, once we were seated. We were sitting close enough for our thighs to be touching as he leaned in, placing his arm around my shoulders.

"I'm not sure why you brought me up here, actually," I answered. He placed his hand on my thigh and I had no desire to move it.

"I want to spend some time with you so that we can get to know each other. I was kicking myself in the ass for letting you walk away without getting your number when we bump into each other earlier," he looked at me so intensely as he spoke. I tried to hold his gaze but couldn't and looked down into my lap before I responded.

"I'm sure a handsome man such as yourself has women lined up trying to get a moment of your time. What is it that you'd like to know about me?" He lifted my chin so that I could look at him again.

"Any and everything that you are willing to share," he spoke with such confidence and it turned me on in the worst way. I smiled but I didn't reply.

"So you're telling me that you didn't feel that connection, that spark when we collided?" he questioned, never taking his eyes off of me. He began running index finger up and down my inner thigh and I could feel that very spark he spoke of.

"Uhh, yeah, I did."

"I had to find out more about you. If I hadn't seen you again tonight, I planned to stalk your floor in your building until I saw you again. I need to see what this is about," he confessed, pointing to me and then himself.

"I'm glad that stalking me isn't going to be necessary. It may have been a little weird," I laughed.

"Maybe. But I would have been smooth with it. You wouldn't have caught on," he chuckled as well, displaying deep dimples in each cheek. I wanted to fan myself but didn't want to let him know how hot he made me feel.

I looked around the VIP area, Candyce and Patryce were occupied with some guys. Patryce happened to look in my direction and gave me the thumbs up motion and Candyce had an annoyed look on her face. I'm not sure if it was for me or the guy who was trying to gain her attention. I didn't really care so I gave my attention back to Malcolm.

"You reserved all of this for your boy's birthday. You're a pretty good friend. You guys must be pretty close."

We looked around and spotted the birthday boy. He had migrated to a seating area directly across from us and seemed to be having a great time. There were scantily clad women flocked around him and I'm sure nothing could wipe the smile from his face.

He shrugged his shoulders and said, "Jordan and I are close, like brothers. But it's not that big of a deal."

"This VIP is everything. Better than any I've ever seen, not that I've seen many. This is actually the first time I've been to this club. It's really nice."

"You don't get out much I guess. I opened this club six months ago," he said casually.

"What? Did you say *you* opened this club six months ago? As in, this is *your* club," I said, very surprised.

"Sure did? Why do you sound so surprised?" he grinned.

"I guess because I am. I don't mean that in a disrespectful way. You look pretty young to be the owner of this club. I'm impressed! It seems to be doing really well. My friends have been here many times and they only have good things to say," I rambled nervously.

"That's good to know. I look young huh? What's young to you?"

"Young to me would be anyone under 30. Although you don't even look that old, honestly," I told him. God I hope this man just looks good for his age.

"Hmm...Interesting. Can I ask what took you so long to visit this club with your girls?" he asked, completely changing the subject of his age.

"No reason, I guess. I just haven't been in the mood to go clubbing," I answered.

"You weren't in the mood to go out and have a good time for six whole months. Do you mind me asking why?"

"Uhh, I had a really bad break up and I was in a funk, I guess. Took me awhile to realize it was his loss."

"His loss, hopefully my gain," he almost whispered. I'm not sure if he meant for me to hear him but I heard him loud and clear. He put his hand up to summon someone from the wait staff. A waitress arrived and he whispered something in her ear

"Yessir, Mr. Bridges. I'll do that right away," she replied to him.

Moments later, several of the wait staff came out with a huge cake, like the kind of cake that a person jumps out of. They rolled it to the section that Jordan and his harem of women were sitting.

On cue, the DJ gave a shout out to Jordan and began to play "Birthday Song" by 2 Chainz. Just like I thought, a woman made her way out of the top of the cake, wearing only a thong and pasties on her breasts. She then proceeded to give Jordan the sexiest lap dance that I've ever seen. I had to look away because watching her made me horny and I am strictly dickly. I'm sure the fact that I haven't had sex in over six months was part of the problem.

"I don't want to be to presumptuous, but I'd like to take you home...to my place," Malcolm whispered with his lips grazing my ear. I guess the lap dance got him horny too.

"Yeah, that is presumptuous of you," I stated and attempted to scoot away from him. It didn't work because he held me in place.

"I don't expect anything from you--," he started to say before I held up my hand and shook my head.

"Look, I don't know you. What makes you think that I'm about to go to your house? That's how people get killed. You could be a killer.

For all you know, I could be a killer. I'm not going to your house," I went off on him. I'm sure that if anyone was looking at us, they thought we were arguing. I had the neck roll and the finger in his face going on.

"I'll come to your place--"

"Okay let's go!" I put my hand over my own mouth in disbelief. It came out before I could even stop it and I noticed the smirk on his face.

We both stood and I made my way over to Patryce and Candyce to let them know that Malcolm was taking me home. Patryce gave me a questioning look and I assured her that I'd be okay. Candyce, of course, had something to say.

"Really Coco," she began, "that's how you doing it. You just met him."

"Don't worry about me Candyce. If something happens to me, I take full responsibility," I told her and walked towards the exit, where Malcolm was waiting.

We made it down the stairs and walked through the main floor of the club. Malcolm stopped and spoke to a few people that worked for him, leaving instructions and letting them know that he was gone for the night. When we got close to the door, Malcolm said that he needed to check something with one of the managers and asked me to wait right here. About thirty seconds after he walked away, I felt someone grab my shoulder pretty roughly, turning me around.

"Hey Coco, I thought that was you. I'm surprised to see you out. How have you been?" It was Jason. My asshole of an ex. He was leaning in too damn close to me because of the loud music and I wanted to chop him in his throat for touching me.

"I've been fine. It was nice to see you," I lied and began to turn away from him to see if I could spot Malcolm. Jason pulled me back.

"Hey, what's the rush. Can I get a dance? You know I miss you," he pulled me and pressed his body up against mine. "You know, your pussy is still the best I've ever had. I know she misses me too," he tried to put his hand under the hem of my dress and I pushed him away and smacked the shit out of him.

"What the fuck is your problem Jason?" I yelled. He held his face in the spot where my hand landed. Just as Jason was about to react, Malcolm stepped in between us.

"Is there a problem here?" he asked Jason, sizing him up.

"Naw, me and my girl just had a little disagreement. We're good, right baby?" Jason said.

"Nigga, I'm not your girl. You got a whole wife at home. Next time you see me, act like you don't!" I screamed and marched out of the main doors of the club. Malcolm wasn't far behind me.

"Let's go," he said, directing me to the Benz that sat waiting in front of us. He walked me to the passenger side and opened the door and made sure I secured my seatbelt before closing it and walking over to the driver side. When he opened his door, I could see security dragging Jason out of the club. *He's such an asshole!*

The first few minutes of the ride were quiet. Jason had completely ruined my mood. For about three seconds, I began to regret inviting this man, that I don't even know, back to my place. However, I looked over at his fine ass and those regrets immediately disappeared.

"Was that the infamous ex?" Malcolm asked when he caught me staring at him.

"Yes, that was his ignorant ass!"

"If it makes you feel any better, he's no longer welcome at the club," he shared.

"That's good to know, if I decide to go there again."

"You will," he said with confidence as he turned and gave me a wink.

"What makes you think I'll go back?" I asked.

"I just have a feeling."

We drove the rest of the way in silence. I didn't need to give him directions because he already knew where I lived. The closer we got to my condo, second thoughts began to creep in again. The little voice inside my head had me questioning what the hell I was thinking.

"You never told me your age," I finally spoke as he pulled into a parking spot in front of my building.

"Does it really matter? I'm legal," he replied with a smirk.

"I don't know if this is a good idea. Legal could mean you just turned twenty-one. I am thirty-nine years old," I began to wonder if he was even thirty since he wasn't forthcoming with his age.

"That's cool. Let me walk you up though," he replied nonchalantly.

He got out and came over to my door. He helped me out and kept ahold of my hand as we made our way to my building.

"Give me your keys." he said when we approached the door.

I took them out of my clutch and handed them to him. He unlocked the door, allowing me to enter first and followed me to the elevator.

"Do you have plans tomorrow? I'd like to take you out," he asked as he stood across from me, undressing me with his eyes.

"That would be nice. Are you talking breakfast, lunch, or dinner?"

We arrived on my floor and stepped off the elevator. He didn't know where my place was so I grabbed his hand and he followed my lead.

When we arrived in front of my door, I stopped, while he unlocked it. He handed me my keys as we stood in front of the door.

"Are you going to answer me?" I asked.

"Whatever works for you," he put his arm up above his head, leaned against the wall and moved his face close to mine.

"Okay, how about….," before I could finish, his lips were on mine. My pussy purred when he kissed my hand but now she is screaming.

He pulled my body against his by the waist and I wrapped my arms around his neck. His tongue engulfed my mouth and I happily made room. I released a soft moan and pressed my body closer to his.

I felt him remove a hand from my ass and fumble with the door handle. Slowly he walked me backwards into my condo. Once we were both inside, I felt him reach behind him and push door closed, followed by the lock. Our lips never parted.

Malcolm reached underneath my dress and yanked my underwear, tearing them away from my body. Our mouths finally parted and he moved down to my neck. His hand moved to my wet box. Instinctively, I wrapped my legs around his waist and he gripped my ass as he pushed forward.

He somehow found the nearest wall and pressed my back against it. With his hands now free, he hoisted my dress over my hips, up my abdomen, leaving it bunched up underneath my breast. Finally, for the first time since our lips met, he disconnected his lips from my body and looked into my eyes.

"Can I have you?"

"Yes!" I responded before he attacked my mouth again with his.

Our kiss became so aggressive that I found myself gasping for air. When he decided to come up for air, he shuffled over to my dining room table, with my legs still wrapped tightly around his waist. He gently placed me on the table, grabbed my knees and pushed my legs open.

I looked up at him and he slowly licked his lips. The look on his face let me know that his tongue was about to have me climbing walls. I didn't have time to prepare myself before he dove his face into my pussy. His tongue swiped up and down feverishly against my clit. It's been so long since she's had any attention that it only took me thirty seconds to release my juices all over his face.

"Oh my damn!" I screamed as I attempted to close my legs but couldn't because of Malcolm's grip on the inside of my thighs.

The fact that I had climaxed meant nothing to him. He continued to indulge in my sweetness until I begged him to stop. His tongue took ownership of every nook and cranny of my honey pot.

"Malcolm, please," I whined as my abdomen contracted, the walls of my pussy pulsed, and my lady juices flowed from my body.

"Please what?" he mumbled against my lower lips.

"I can't take it!" I yelled as I pushed his head away.

He finally had mercy on me and came up for air. I tried to sit up but was too weak and Malcolm realized that and lifted me from the table, bridal style, allowing me to wrap my arms around his neck.

"Where's your bedroom?" he whispered. I answered him but I'm not so sure what I said. My condo had two bedrooms and he managed to find the master.

Placing me on the bed, he lifted each leg, one at a time, and removed my shoes. My dress was still hiked up under my breasts and he lifted it the rest of the way, over my head. I now lay, naked before him, because I didn't have on a bra. His eyes gazed over my body and he reached down to grab his dick.

He kicked off his shoes and quickly removed his clothing, down to his boxers. They looked like a tent because his member stood at attention. From what I could see, the Lord had definitely blessed him.

"You ready?"

I couldn't find my voice so I swallowed and nodded my head.

"I want to hear you say it. Tell me you want this dick!" he demanded as he stepped out of his boxers.

I do want the dick. But I'm speechless right now. I've never seen a man so well-endowed in real life. I'm seriously wondering if my pussy can handle this man.

"Uhh, I," I began.

"You what Coco?" he asked as he stroked himself. I got so turned on watching him that I had to squeeze my legs together.

"I want the dick!" I finally declared.

"Good! Because I'm about to fuck up your whole world."

He retrieved his wallet from his pants and got a condom. Once he covered himself, he leaned down and left a trail of kisses from my stomach to my mouth. This man's tongue was magical and he knew how to use it to bring out sensations that I've never experienced with anyone else.

I was so enthralled with his tongue in my mouth, then my earlobe, then my neck, I didn't notice that he put the head of his penis at my opening. In one quick movement that damn near sent me over the edge, he pushed his way into my slippery walls.

"Shit!" I screamed just before he covered my mouth with his again.

His thrusts started out slow and thorough. When I say thorough, I mean he pushed himself deep inside of me before pulling almost all the way out. I could feel every inch of him as he glided in and out.

"Mmm, shit!" Malcolm moaned into my neck. "This pussy is the truth, baby, damn."

My mind is in a frenzy. I can't think. My body is tingling all over. Never in my life has a man fucked me like this. I don't want this to end but I feel my senses reaching their limit. My orgasm is near and it's gonna be explosive.

"Malcolm, baby, I'm abo---, fuuuccckkk! I'm cuummin got dammit!" I screamed so loud that I'm expecting my neighbors to be looking at me funny tomorrow.

Malcolm didn't ease up one bit. He was relentless in his attack on my pussy. His strokes somehow felt deeper, longer, and harder. I feel like I'm having an outer body experience.

I've never had back-to-back orgasms. But today is clearly a day for first. First time ever bringing a nigga to my house that I just met, first one night stand, first time I've had my pussy eaten on my dining room table, and first back-to-back orgasms. I guess there's a first time for everything. As my next orgasm hit, it's also the first time I saw heaven.

"Ahhhh, fuck! Oh my God Malcolm!" I cried. When he told me he was about to fuck up my whole world, I thought it was just him being cocky and overconfident. But he did that and then some.

Then I heard something that sounded so guttural, so animalistic, so...satisfied, as Malcolm released his seeds into the condom.

"Damn," Malcolm mumbled. His breathing was labored, as was mine. He shifted his body to the side, to relieve some of his weight from my body.

"Malcolm, how old are you?" I asked again, hoping he would tell me and that he met my minimum age requirement for men that I date.

"Twenty-five."

Fuck!

****

The next morning, I woke up to the smell of bacon. *What the hell?* I sat up and tried to get my bearings. *I'm in my condo, in my bed. Who the hell?* I looked around my room to see if I could find a clue as to who is in my kitchen cooking. My eyes landed on his shirt first, then his jeans. *Oh shit.* Malcolm!

Then it all came rushing back to me. The twenty-five year old that fucked up my whole world with the most amazing sex I've had in my life. I attempted to quickly get out of my bed to take care of my hygiene but the soreness between my legs reminded me Malcolm's master skills. Instead, I eased my way out of bed and slowly made my way to my bathroom. After washing my face and brushing my teeth, I slipped on my satin robe and went to the kitchen.

At first, Malcolm didn't notice me. I couldn't help but smile as I watched him, in his boxer briefs, dance around my kitchen with my pink headphones on, preparing what looked to be a breakfast fit for a queen. The sight of him had my pussy thumping and I had to squeeze my thighs together. I actually moaned out loud. *Lawd why does he have to be so young? This will never work.*

He finally turned in my direction and noticed me standing there and smiled immediately. He pulled the headphones from his ears with his one free hand and put the orange juice on the counter that he was holding with the other.

"C'mere beautiful," he reached his hand out for me. I went to him and he pulled me into his arms, wrapping his arms around my waist.

"Good afternoon," he kissed me on my forehead. "I didn't think you were ever gon' wake up. Do you always sleep this late?" He looked into my eyes and I was so mesmerized that I couldn't respond. So my crazy ass just smiled.

"You good?" he asked when I didn't say anything.

"Huh? Oh yeah. I'm fine," I finally responded. "What time is it anyway?"

"One o'clock," he replied.

"Oh my God. I don't know how I slept this late. I rarely sleep past eight on weekends. Regardless of what time I go to bed," I answered, shocked at how late in the day it was.

"I guess you had a long and tiring night." He winked and smirked at me before releasing me from his hold.

"I'm sure you're hungry, after the night you had. Have a seat and let me fix your plate," he continued to tease me then began moving around the kitchen, like he was at home.

"Are you still tired baby? Have a seat, I'll bring you your food," he told me again because I seemed to be frozen in place.

My feet eventually listened to my brain and took me to the table and I sat down and waited to be served. *This is new. I've never had a man cook for me or serve me. He can't be twenty-five.*

He made few trips back and forth from the table to the kitchen. When he finally sat next to me, the table had plates and bowls filled with Belgium waffles, scrambled eggs, bacon, and lastly pineapples and strawberries. He filled two glasses with orange juice and proceeded to make my plate. When he finished, he grabbed my hand and prayed over the food. *Where did this man/child come from?*

"Eat up beautiful," he said before he dug in.

I must have been in a trance. I sat there in awe of the person before me. There had to be a catch. After he feeds me, he's going to cut me up and feed me to the pitbulls that he's raising in his basement.

"Coco?" he called my name, getting my attention.

I shook my head to clear it of the crazy thoughts and put a spoon full eggs in my mouth.

"Where did all of this food come from? I desperately need to go grocery shopping."

He laughed before answering. "Yeah, I noticed that. I had some groceries delivered. There should be enough to last you about a week or so."

"What? Are you serious?"

"I am. I hope the items I chose are to your liking."

"I, um, I'm sure they are. I'm not picky. Thank you. You, umm, you didn't have to do that," I am just stunned. He probably thinks I'm an idiot. I haven't been able to string together two coherent sentences since I got out of bed. *What the hell is wrong with me?*

"It was my pleasure. Now, eat up," he waited to take another bite of his food for me to start eating.

The rest of the meal was eaten pretty much in silence. Clearly, my communication skills are lacking this afternoon so I didn't even attempted to start a conversation.

Once we finished eating, do you know this nigga told me to go shower while he cleaned the kitchen? *Again, I ask, where the hell did he come from?* If my body wasn't so sore from him "fucking up my world"

I would think that I was dreaming and he was a figment of my imagination.

After my shower, I put on some lounge shorts and a tank top since I didn't know our plans. When I walked out of my bedroom, he came out of the second bathroom looking good enough to eat. He had showered and put on some basketball shorts, that hung just low enough for me to see his v-cut...and his dick print. *Down girl, I told my pussy.* Since he wasn't wearing a shirt, I could see his tattoos. *Damn this nigga is fine! But he's only twenty-five!*

"So what's the plan?" I asked, ignoring my thoughts.

"You wanna Netflix and chill?" he joked.

"Actually, there are a few movies on Netflix that I have been wanting to watch."

"Let's do it. I got popcorn and some movie candy."

"Oh, you just have everything planned out. How do you know I wasn't going to kick you out?" I playfully pushed him in the shoulder.

"Cause I put this good dick on you, that's how," he winked and went to the kitchen to get our movie snacks ready.

The dick was more than good. It was amazing. While he was in the kitchen, I turned on the T.V. and connected to Netflix to find our first movie.

By the time he came back to the living room, I had a movie ready. We sat next to each other on the couch and I grabbed a blanket. He pulled me to his side and I snuggled up next to him. *This is perfect.*

The next four days were unbelievable. We spent it watching movies on Netflix and getting to know each other. I work for myself and did some work from home. Malcolm made a lot of phone calls to ensure his business was taken care of. We talked about everything under the sun, from our childhood and teen years, our families, our likes and dislikes, past relationships, and anything else you could think of, including sharing our HIV/STD results. I know more about Malcolm than I did about my last three boyfriends.

We had sex in every room in my condo, on every surface that it was possible to do so. It was the most amazing, blissful, and fulfilling time of my life and I didn't want it to end. With each passing moment, each conversation, each meal that he made for me, each bath that her ran for me, each mind-blowing orgasm, I think I fell in love. *But it's only been four days Coco. And he's twenty-five.*

On the fifth day, something in the air shifted. As his tongue took hostage of my slippery center, bringing me closer and closer to my climax, I turned my brain off and allowed my heart takeover. The sensations that my body felt as his mouth caressed my lower lips seemed unreal.

"Shit baby, it feels so good," I panted, barely able to breath because I could feel my orgasm building in the pits of my stomach.

He released a moan, letting me know that he heard me. "Oh God Malcolm, I'm cummin'." My pussy released the juices that he was searching for all over his face.

Without giving me a moment to catch my breath, Malcolm slid up my body and pushed his dick inside of me.

"Ah fuck!" he grunted as my walls made room for him.

He gyrated his hips as if he was on a mission. His balls slapped against my ass as he dipped his hips in and out of the apex of my thighs.

"Damn, I love you!" I confessed. Forgetting that I've only known him for five days. Forgetting that he was only twenty-five. Forgetting that my friends and family won't agree with our relationship. Forgetting any and everything that went against what my heart was telling me.

He lifted his head from my neck and looked into my eyes before confessing, "I love you too."

Our mouths connected in an earth-shattering kiss. His tongue devoured mine as if he was trying to communicate his love for me. I could feel it. No kiss from any man I've ever been with felt like this. No man has ever made me feel like this. I'm ready and willing to risk it all.

When he released my tongue from hostage, he began to grind his hips deeper, faster, and harder. My pussy pulsed as I got closer to the finish line and I could feel his rod pulsing inside of me.

"Marry me," he said as we came together. "Marry me Coco."

"Okay," I whispered. "I'll marry you."

You could only hear our breathing as we deescalated from our high. *Does he know what he just asked me? Is my pussy that good? Did I just agree to marry him?*

"Let's go to Vegas. Tonight. I want you to be my wife and I don't want to wait."

The look in his eyes was so sincere. The urgency in his voice told me that he meant every word.

"Let's do it!"

THE END

7 TIME TABLE

"Baby, did Sam say who all they invited over tonight?" my wife of three months, Janelle, called out from our bathroom.

"Not really. I know the usual people but he did mention that a few new people would be there. Some people Mia knows," I replied to her.

"New people huh? Well, I'm almost ready. Give me ten more minutes baby."

"I don't know why you're getting all dolled up anyway. We're just chilling at Sam and Mia's house," I fussed.

"I'm not getting all dolled up but I washed my hair. You know it takes me forever to tame it." She wasn't lying about that. My wife has some of the thickest, curliest hair I've ever seen on a woman. She mostly wears it up in a ball on the top of her head. Wearing it out frustrated her, she said, but I love it.

"Baby, just wear it out. You know I love that shit. Then when we get home I can pull on it while I'm hittin' it from the back." I went in the bathroom, walked up behind her, wrapped my arms around her waist and began kissing her neck.

She stopped what she was doing with her hair and turned her face towards mine to kiss my lips.

"As much as I would enjoy that, I'm not wearing it out tonight. It'll take even longer to get ready if I do that anyway. But you can still hit it from the back when we get home," she said as she rubbed her ass on my dick.

"If you keep playin' I'm gon' bend you over right here, right now," I slapped her on her ass before walking out of the bathroom.

"Ouch baby, that hurt," she yelled after me.

"Quit whining and hurry up baby."

Twenty minutes later we were walking out of the door. Sam and Mia live about twenty minutes away from us. We started having game night a few years ago, meeting once or twice a month, depending on our schedules. Things have changed so much since then, with some of us being in relationships and some not anywhere close to settling down. When we arrived, not too many cars were there so we weren't too late.

"I wonder who these new people are that Mia invited. She's always trying to invite outside people," Janelle fussed while we waited for someone to answer the door.

"Be nice baby," I smiled at her and shook my head. Janelle and Mia are cool, I would say they are good friends but they aren't extremely close. They spend a lot of time together by default because Sam, Mia's husband, is my best friend.

"I'm always nice. I just don't get why she's always trying to introduce more people into our crew. Remember the last girl that Mia brought around almost got her ass beat by Leah for trying to fuck with Shawn," Janelle reminded me. That was some funny shit. Leah had that girl running out of the house with no shoes on in the snow.

"Yeah, well hopefully that won't happen again," I said as I lifted my hand to press the doorbell again.

"Hey guys! Come on in!" Mia said when she opened the door.

We walked in and exchanged pleasantries. "Everyone is in the basement. I'm just hanging out up here making sure the food is good to go and waiting for a few more people," Mia told us and headed back to the kitchen.

"Baby go ahead down. I'll wait up here with Mia."

"Your ass just trying to be nosy," she laughed because she knew I was right. I kissed her forehead and went to the basement.

I walked down the stairs that led to the basement. As I got close to the bottom of the stairs, I heard some of the conversation that they were having.

"The past is the past. My current man doesn't need to know how many men I was with before him or who they were for that matter. Why would he need to know any of that?" I recognized that as Khloe's voice.

"Because don't no man want a woman with a high body count and most men don't want to fuck with somebody that their homie done fucked!"

That was Xavier. He is the notoriously single guy of the group. I don't think he can keep a woman for more than a month. He claims that he isn't looking to settle down but we all know that he's such an asshole that not settling down isn't his choice.

I walked around to the lounging area and made my presence known. "What the hell are ya'll debating about today?" I interrupted, even though I knew what the topic of discussion was.

"Now here's a man with some common sense. Ask him," Khloe said and all eyes turned towards me.

"Isaiah, did you ever ask Janelle how many niggas she fucked before you?" Xavier's old tactless ass asked me.

"The fuck? Why the hell would I wanna know that? Some shit is better left unsaid!" I replied.

"Man, come on! You mean to tell me that you've never wondered how many niggas been up in your woman. Or if she fucked any of the homie's?" Xavier pressed. See what I mean, he's an asshole.

"Nope because when they had it, it wasn't mine. I don't give a damn. Nigga you stupid!" I shook my head and walked over to the bar to grab a beer out of the fridge they had down there.

Just then, Janelle, Mia, and a few others entered the basement. Janelle walked over to me and grabbed my beer. She took a sip and gave me a look of disgust before giving it back to me. She's not really a drinker, especially not beer.

"That's what you get," I laughed and gave her a peck on the lips. She turned her back to me and I pulled her close as we stood behind the bar area.

"Hey everyone," Mia began, "this is a friend from work, Michelle and her boyfriend Mark. And this is Michelle's cousin, Tiana."

I wasn't paying attention during the first part of the introduction because Janelle was rubbing her ass against my growing dick. But when I heard Mia introduce Tiana, I looked up. *Shit!*

Everyone went around the room introducing themselves and when it got to Janelle and I, Janelle said, "This is my husband---"

"Isaiah, good to see you again," Tiana interrupted as she walked in our direction.

Janelle looked, turned her head up and back to get a good look at me and questioned, "You know her?"

"Ummm---" I started.

"Yeah, he knows me. Pretty well actually. We dated for a bit." Tiana finished and gave me a sly look.

The whole basement was quiet, as they waited to see how this played out.

"Oh really? Small world," Janelle said, folding her arms across her chest, defensively.

"Yeah, it is. How long have you two been married?" Tiana asked.

"Three months," Janelle and I both answered.

"Aww, newlyweds. Isn't that cute?" Tiana said, sarcastically.

I could tell by the way Tiana was looking that she was trying to start some shit. *This ain't gonna end well.*

"Is there a problem?" Janelle asked as she turned and directed an evil glare towards me.

"Naw baby," I grabbed her hands and kissed each of them. "Why would there be a problem?"

"I'm sensing some tension between ya'll. So, is there a problem?" Janelle asked again, this time looking at Tiana.

"Hey Janelle! Can you help me start bringing the food down?" Mia marched over to us and pulled her in the direction of the stairs.

I was thanking my lucky stars for Mia at that moment. Janelle went with her with no objections but if looks could kill, Tiana's ass would be dead as hell. Shit, I don't think it's looking good for me either.

As soon as they were upstairs, Xavier, Sam, and one of my other homie, Jeff, were in my face.

"So, what's up with you and Tiana?" Xavier started the interrogation.

"Fuck you mean? Ain't shit up with us!" I defended.

"Let me ask it another way," Sam intervened. "Did you hit that?"

"Oh, he did more that hit it," Tiana added, smugly, forcing herself into our space.

"Yo, don't do that. You know it wasn't even like that with us," I reminded her.

Tiana's cousin Michelle and her boyfriend made their way to where we were standing near the bar.

"Is this the nigga that you said just up and went ghost on you cousin?" Michelle asked laced with attitude.

"Baby, stay out of this shit. This ain't got nothin' to do with you," her boyfriend Mark warned her.

"If it involves my cousin, it involves me so---," Michelle continued.

"No the fuck it don't!" Mark slightly raised his voice and gave her a look. She shut the hell up after that.

Before we could continue, Mia, Janelle and Leah came back down to the basement with platters of food.

"Sam, can you guys go grab the other stuff?" Mia asked.

"Yeah baby," he replied as all guys followed him upstairs.

Xavier's nosy ass couldn't wait to ask more questions. "Why you all close-mouthed nigga? Give us the details."

"There are no details nosy ass! We used to fuck around. I got with Janelle and ended shit with Tiana. Simple as that!" I explained, although I did leave out a few key parts.

"You must have left one heck of an impression with the shade she was just throwing," Sam added.

"Guess so," I agreed as we went back downstairs. I don't want to talk about this subject anymore.

We walked over to the bar area and placed the food on the counter where the ladies had the other food. I looked around to see where Janelle was and she stood in the corner with Leah, mean mugging Tiana, who was on the other side of the room.

"Baby, you want me to fix you a plate?" I called out to her.

"I wouldn't think you were such a gentlemen, the way you just up and disappeared on a bitch," Tiana interrupted before Janelle could answer.

"Look, I gave your ass a pass earlier with the shade you were trying to throw. But your passes have run out," Janelle said as she slowly walked over to Tiana.

I quickly made my way from behind the bar and wrapped my arms around Janelle's shoulders.

"Baby ---," I started.

"Naw don't baby me," she stopped me and then directed her statement to Tiana. "I don't have a problem with the fact that ya'll used to fuck. But I'm not feeling your whole attitude towards me," Janelle said to Tiana.

"Maybe if you knew that your husband was fucking us both at the same time you'd understand why I have an attitude," Tiana threw back at her.

"Hold the fuck up. Don't start lying and shit!" I defended.

"I don't have a reason to lie?" She looked at me with a raised brow.

"Obviously you don't need a reason. The fuck you mean?" Tiana done pissed me off now. Part of the reason I could never be in a serious relationship with her is because she's so damn messy. All she had to offer was pussy.

Everyone in the room was quiet as hell. It was like me, Janelle and Tiana were the only ones in the room.

Tiana walked over to where Janelle and I stood and whipped out her phone, turning her body so that Janelle and I could see her screen.

After unlocking it, she went to her text messages and searched my name. The string of messages popped up and she scrolled down to the last one that I sent. The date read Friday, June 16, 2017. *Shit.*

"I'm gone," Janelle snatched her purse from the couch and stomped up the stairs. Her and I made shit official on June 17th, which is Janelle's birthday. Although we hadn't had the conversation, she thought that she was the only person that I was seeing before that.

"Baby wait!" I went after her.

When I got upstairs, the door was open and I heard the screen door slam. "Janelle, baby wait," I got outside and she was already in the driver seat of my car. By the time I reached the passenger door, she damn near ran over my toes when she pulled off.

"Fuck!" I yelled as I ran my hand down my face.

I pulled out my phone and called Janelle several times but she kept sending me to voicemail. I stayed outside for a few minutes trying to figure out what the hell just happened. I also needed to calm down because I wanted to wrap my hands around Tiana's neck.

When I went back inside and to the basement, all eyes were on me. My eyes landed on Tiana, as she stood there with a smirk on her face. I started in her direction but Sam must have sensed what I had on my mind and got between us before I could choke her ass up.

"Hold up man! I can't let you do that!" Sam said, lightly pushing me back.

"This broad just waltzed her ass up in here and single-handedly tried to fuck up my marriage. Why the fuck would you do that? I don't owe you shit!" I shouted to Tiana.

"Because you just up and disappeared. I tried to contact you on numerous occasions and you had me blocked on everything I tried," she screamed.

"So the fuck what! I guess you finally got the hint that I was done fucking with you and had moved on. That still doesn't explain the point you were trying to make showing all that shit to my wife."

"Well if you wouldn't have gone ghost on a bitch you would know that you have a three-month-old son!" she spat and folded her arms across her chest.

"What!"

"What the hell!"

"Aww hell naw!"

Everyone in the room was shocked by her statement. I stood frozen, hoping that I didn't hear her correctly.

"Okay! Party's over. Ya'll ain't got to go home but ya'll got to get up outta here. Feel free to take a to-go plate but ya'll gotta go," Sam said as he ushered people towards the food and the stairs.

"What did you say?"

"I said that you have a three-month-old son. Believe me, had it not been for him, I would have quickly forgotten about your mediocre ass dick." She threw more shade but I let her slide.

"That's not possible!" I yelled. "There's no way!" I sat on the nearest couch and put my hands on either side of my head.

"Aye man! Let me get all of these people out of here so you can have some privacy while you discuss this. Just chill," Sam offered.

I sat in disbelief as Sam's guests gathered food and left. About ten minutes later, Tiana and I were alone in the basement. At first, neither of us said a word.

"Tiana, I realize that I didn't end things with us the right way. But trying to pin a baby on me is not the way to go," I finally spoke.

"Isaiah, I liked you but I wasn't in love. I can be a lil ratchet but I ain't that damn ratchet. I wouldn't do no shit like that," Tiana defended.

"I can't tell with the shit you just pulled in front of my wife and all these other damn people!" I yelled.

"I ain't gon' lie. It kinda hurt my feelings knowing that you were married and I had to go through my whole pregnancy and the last three months without the father of my child," she admitted.

"I wrapped up every time we had sex and ---," I reasoned.

"And condoms break. They aren't a hundred percent. Look, let's just get a DNA test. I'm not about to argue with you about what I know is true."

"Fine! I'll unblock your number. Send me the details," I said as I got up and went upstairs, with Tiana following me.

Sam, Mia, Michelle and her boyfriend Mark were the only people still present. I guess they were Tiana's ride home. I realized that I no longer had a way home and pulled out my phone to request an Uber.

"You good?" Sam asked.

"No but um, I just ordered an Uber. I'm gonna wait outside," I told him and headed towards the door.

"Aww man, I can take you home. It's no biggie," Sam offered, grabbing my shoulder.

"Naw, I need some time alone. Thanks though," I declined and went to wait outside.

I have no idea how in the hell I'm gonna tell Janelle that there is a possibility that I have a son. It's not like I can keep it from her until the DNA test comes back either. Everybody at the party heard Tiana's confession. *Shit! I'm screwed!*

About twenty minutes later, the Uber driver pulled up at my house. I could only hope that Janelle was home and hadn't ran off somewhere.

When I walked into the house, it was dark, but I could see Janelle's purse on the bench in the entryway. *Thank God!*

I threw my keys on the kitchen table and went directly to our bedroom. When I twisted the knob and tried to push the door open, I almost broke my nose because it was locked.

"Jay, baby, open the door!" I yelled and knocked at the same time. I waited a few beats before I tried again.

"Janelle, open the door baby. We need to talk this shit out. Just let me explain," I pleaded.

Still nothing. I guess she wants me to act a damn fool. I have no problem kicking this door down.

"Jay, you know I will kick this damn door down so why don't you save me the trouble and us the money and open the door baby?"

I heard some movement behind the door just before I heard it unlock. I tried the knob and thankfully my baby wasn't too mad to hear me out.

"Say what the fuck you have to say, Isaiah, so you can get the fuck out," she walked over to the bed and sat with her arms folded and one leg folded underneath her.

"Baby, you know I love you and only you," I began. She rolled her eyes and blew out a deep breath. It hurt that she didn't even care to look at me while I spoke.

"Listen, when we first started dating, I was trickin' off a lil bit," I began again.

"Clearly," she said, sarcastically.

I reached out to grab her hand and she snatched away from me. I let out a breath and continued.

"I didn't cut off the others until I knew that I wanted to be committed to you and---,"

"So you were fucking me and them?" She asked.

"No, well, yeah, I mean, kind of," I stammered as she shook her head in disgust. I slowly moved closer to her, not knowing what her reaction would be. When she didn't move or swing on me, I sat next to her on the bed and turned her body towards mine and kept my hands on her shoulders.

"It wasn't like that baby. I wasn't sleeping with any of them okay. Except Tiana. But as soon as you and me had the exclusivity discussion, I cut her off. I blocked her number and I didn't see or talk to her again until today."

"That doesn't make it any better. You were cheating on me!" She cried.

"I know that's what it seems like but technically…" I paused because she looked up at me with so much hurt in her eyes.

"Technically Isaiah. That's how you're going to explain yourself. By saying "technically" we weren't exclusive so it wasn't cheating?" She got up and paced the floor in front of the bed.

"Well---," I began.

"Well nothing! What if I told you that I was still fucking one of my fuck buddies before we became exclusive? How would you feel about that Isaiah?" she yelled while she poked me in the chest with her index finger.

"I wouldn't be happy about it but how could I be mad. Listen, once we made it official, I cut everybody off. Just know that since that moment, it's been me and you. I would never do anything to hurt you intentionally baby. I love you too much to do that. You're my wife now Jay. I'm not about to let some shit that went down before you were my girl tear us apart. Now stop trippin'."

I got up from the bed and walked over to her, grabbing her wrist, pulling her to me, then wrapping my arm around her waist. "I need you to forgive me okay. I'm sorry that I was on some creep shit for a minute but it didn't take me long to realize that you were who I wanted to spend the rest of my life with," I continued to plead my case.

I could tell from the way she looked at me that she was softening up. "Do you forgive me?" I kissed her forehead, then her nose, then finally her lips.

She looked up at me with her big doe-shaped eyes and her curly hair all over her head. She really has no choice but to forgive a nigga cause I'm never letting her go.

"I forgive you but I'm still hurt. This bitch just came out of nowhere with this shit and it caught me by surprise. I don't like people telling me shit about my man that I don't already know."

"I get it and I'm sorry baby," I kissed her again and pushed my tongue into her mouth. I was surprised and grateful that she allowed it. This is our first big argument since we've been married. I actually don't recall us ever beefing about anything serious since we've been together.

While our tongues danced around each other, I stuck my hands down the back of the leggings that she had changed into and gripped her ass, thankful that she rarely wore underwear.

My mouth made its way down to her neck and she moaned so softly that I could barely hear it. That's how she is when she calls herself having an attitude with me. She doesn't want me to know that she wants the dick just as much as I want to give it to her, so she tries to muffle her moans.

"You know you want this dick Jay, why you playing?" I said between kissing and sucking on her neck.

I backed her up against our bed and she fell back on it, automatically opening her legs which allowed me to lie between them. With my hands still in her pants, gripping her ass, I pushed her pelvis against mine as she grinded in circles. Those moans that she tried to stifle became louder.

I moved one of my hands around to the front and brushed my fingers against her clit. Janelle was always wet for me. I inserted two fingers inside of her throbbing walls and pressed my thumb against her clit.

"Ahh!" she called out.

My mouth covered hers again and we kissed passionately while I fingered her to climax.

"I'm about to cum baby!" she cried out.

I increased the speed and pressure of my fingers and Janelle came all over my hand. I pulled my hand from her pants and licked my fingers. She always tasted so sweet. I stood and removed my shirt, pants and boxers. My dick sprang free and I saw Janelle lick her lips.

When she sat up, my dick got harder because I knew she was about to suck the soul out of my dick. Janelle gave the best head I've ever had. She reached for my rod and wrapped her soft, small hands around it. Using her thumb, she rubbed the pre-cum around the head. I felt her pull me gently towards her and I took a few steps until her mouth and my dick were aligned.

Using her tongue, Janelle teased the tip of my dick before engulfing it in her mouth. The warmth and wetness had me ready to bust almost immediately.

"Shit!" I groaned as my fingers became intertwined in her hair.

Her mouth slid up and down my member as she used her tongue to make circles around the head each time she pulled back. I held her head steady as she allowed me to fuck her mouth and soon I felt my nut rising. My baby has no problem swallowing but I want to bust this nut inside of her pussy and not her mouth. When I tell her about this baby she might leave a nigga. But if she's pregnant, that's another story.

I pulled my dick out of her mouth and she looked at me like I was crazy. "I need to be inside of you now! Turn around and put that ass in the air for me," I commanded.

She smiled and did just as I asked. My baby had the perfect waist-to-ass ratio so when I hit it from the back, my hands gripped her hips perfectly. As soon as she was in position, her pussy was like a magnet to my dick, pulling me inside.

"Ah fuck!" I growled. My dick fit inside of her walls like a glove.

Janelle was playing no games with me tonight. She threw her ass back as I pounded her from behind. The sound of her ass cheeks smacking against my pelvis as my dick slid in and out of her was music to my ears.

"Shit baby, keep throwin' that ass back. Just like that baby," I reached around her and rubbed on her clit. I need her to cum because the way she's handling my dick, I'm sure I won't last much longer.

"Fuck, baby, I'm cumin'!" she screamed.

"Cum on yo dick baby! Wet it up!" I coaxed her.

As always, her pussy was obedient and I felt her walls clutch me like a vice grip. We hadn't agreed that we were trying for a baby, even though Janelle is not on birth control and we stopped using condoms. My pull out game is strong. But not today.

"Got damn!" I groaned into her back as I released my seeds inside of her.

"You ready to have my baby Jay?" I asked between placing kisses on her back.

"Fuck Isaiah! You didn't pull out!" She began to squirm but I had a tight grip on her and my dick was still inside of her.

"It felt too good baby. I thought we said if it happens it happens. What's the problem?" I asked, kissing the side of her neck.

"Nothing, let me up."

I slowly slid my dick from its home and my shit was still rock hard. "Baby, he's not done. Where you going?"

"Too bad. I'm going to shower," she got up and switched her fine ass to the bathroom.

"Okay, round two in the shower," I said and followed her to the bathroom. I'll tell her about my possible baby in the morning.

****

"You asshole! I can't believe you did this to me!" I heard Janelle screaming before I felt myself being drenched in cold water.

I quickly sat up in the bed and ran my hand down my face, in an attempt to wipe the water from my eyes. Before I could even process what was going on, I was being hit with something metal and round. I put my hands up to block the object but Janelle had lost her mind.

"Janelle, what the fuck? Calm down," I yelled as I grabbed whatever she was hitting me with and threw it to the other side of the room.

"You want me to calm down! Did you forget to tell me something last night nigga?" She no longer had the object in her hand to hit me with so she climbed on the bed and started swinging her fist.

"Jay baby! Please let me explain!" I grabbed her wrists and flipped her over on the bed so that I was on top of her.

"I thought you did all of your explaining last night. But you forgot to tell me the most important detail. How could you? How could you do this to me?" she cried.

"Baby listen. I was gonna tell you this morning. I swear. I don't even know if the kid is mine. Please Jay, you gotta believe me baby," I pleaded.

"I'm your wife. I'm supposed to have all your babies. Get off me Isaiah! I don't even wanna be around you right now. Pack you some shit and go to one of your boy's houses. I don't want you here!" She twisted and turned underneath me to no avail.

"Hell naw! I'm not leaving this house. We not doin' that Jay. This ain't how we gon' handle shit. I'm sorry baby. I swear I am. But we ain't about to be apart. Now I'm about to let you go but you need to calm your ass down and keep them little ass fist to yourself," I slowly got up, keeping my eyes on her the whole time.

Thankfully, she didn't swing on me anymore. This whole time my ass was naked trying to calm her ass down so I went and got some basketball shorts to put on, used the bathroom and took care of my hygiene. When I walked back into our bedroom, Janelle had on some leggings with a hoodie and was stuffing clothes into a duffle bag.

"Hold the fuck up Jay! What are you doing?" I marched over to her and yanked the duffle bag away.

"Since you won't leave, I'm leaving. Now give me back my damn bag!" She reached for it but wasn't quick enough. I held the bag in the air so she couldn't reach it.

"Jay, I'm not playing with you. We not doin' this. What did we say before we got married? What did we promise each other in our premarital classes? This is not how we handle shit. Baby, we don't even know if the baby is mine. Can we confirm that before we make any rash decisions?"

The hurt on my baby's face broke my heart and there wasn't shit that I could do to fix it except pray that the baby isn't mine.

"I need some air!" She turned and stomped out of our room, slamming every door that she went through on the way out of the door. *I hope she comes back.*

*******Two Weeks Later******

The past two weeks have been hell. Janelle agreed not to leave but she got me in the guest room. We've been cordial with each other but I want my wife back. I want to kiss her, wrap my arms around her, just love on her. I can't do this other shit much longer.

"You have mail!" Janelle barked as she threw an envelope on the table and walked away.

I walked over to the table and grabbed the envelope. *Shit!* It's the DNA test results. I've been anxious for and dreading this day at the same time. If I have a seed out there, I definitely want to know about it. But I can't lie, I don't want this baby to be mine.

I took a deep breath and slowly ripped the envelope open and took the folded sheet of paper out. Whatever is on this paper is going to change my life. As I read the results, my eyes became blurry and my breathing picked up. I read it over probably twenty times before I finally went to find Janelle.

When I walked into our bedroom, she was sitting on the chaise with her legs pulled up to her chest, no doubt, waiting for me to tell her the results of the DNA test. The look in her eyes was one of uncertainty and fear. I hate that my actions had her like this.

"Baby, you know I love ---" I began.

"Just tell me the results Isaiah!" she interrupted.

I couldn't look her in the eyes as I told her the results. I just hope we can get back to us.

"He's mine," I whispered.

The sound that came from her was gut-wrenching. I reached out to pull her into a hug and she pushed me away and pounded me on the chest.

"How could you? How could you make a baby with someone else? This isn't how it's supposed be," she cried as her little fist hit me on my chest.

"Baby, I'm so sorry. I didn't do this on purpose. I would never hurt you like this on purpose baby. You gotta believe me."

She pushed me away and walked over to our bed. After pulling the comforter back, she got in and threw the covers over her head. Her sobs broke my heart. I went to her to try and console her but she wanted no parts of me.

"Don't touch me. Just go! I don't want you here right now. Just leave!" she demanded.

I didn't want to leave her. I wanted to take her pain away but I knew there was nothing that I could do. So I left her, for now. But she had another thing coming if she thought we weren't going to work this out.

*******Two Months Later******

A few days after I received the DNA test results, I met up with Tiana in a neighborhood park to meet my son for the first time. If I had seen him before taking the DNA test, the test wouldn't have been necessary. It's crazy how much he looks like me.

My son's name is Israel and I fell in love with him immediately. I never thought that I could have this much love in my heart for anyone besides my wife. He's almost six months old now and is developing his own little personality. It's amazing to see.

Tiana and I have worked out a fair visitation schedule and child support payments. As much as I wanted to be upset with Tiana and how she brought this to me, after thinking about it, I can understand. She definitely showed her ass that day but since then, she hasn't been a problem at all.

Janelle and I are on our way back to being us. The first couple of weeks after we found out that I had a son was rough. She continued to refuse to sit down and have a conversation with me about how we could move forward and I almost said fuck it. But I love my wife too much to allow some shit that went down before we were married, hell, before we were an official couple, fuck up my marriage.

She cut herself off from all of our family and friends and the only thing she did was go to work, then come home and close herself up in our room. Finally, her mother got fed up with not being able to reach her and came to our house. Damn did the shit hit the fan.

Janelle's mom is a no nonsense kind of woman. She let Janelle have it! I had repeatedly apologized to Janelle and tried to reason with her about the time table of when my son was conceived. She didn't want to listen to anything I said to her. But after I explained everything to her mom, Mama Jenkins told her about herself.

In a nutshell, Mama Jenkins told Janelle that she was being selfish, unreasonable, immature, and just plain dumb, if she allowed this situation to ruin her marriage. She said a lot of other stuff too and I felt bad for my wife but I was happy that her mom understood my side of the story.

"What's wrong with him?" Janelle asked, interrupting my reflection. As soon as she came into the den, she reached for Israel, who was whining for no damn reason that I could figure out.

"I don't know. He's been cranky since I picked him up from daycare," I told her and passed him to her.

"Heyyy, what's wrong with Jay's Izzyboo?" she cooed and kissed him on the cheeks. He instantly calmed down for her.

I was completely surprised at Janelle's total change in attitude. I know a lot of what her mom said hit home and contributed to her change of heart. I also know that the first time she saw Israel, she loved him. The hurt, pain and fear that I saw in her eyes for weeks was immediately gone. She loved my son as if he were her own and for that, I am thankful.

"I done told you about calling him that girly shit Jay."

"Oh hush! He may be teething," she suggested as she let him gnaw on her finger.

"Oh, I guess that could be it. Tiana didn't mention anything about that."

Janelle and Tiana's relationship is getting better as time progresses. Understandably, Jay has some issues because of how Tiana came into our lives. But Tiana has apologized for that and they are cool. I don't expect them ever to be besties but for the sake of Israel, they are making it work.

"Can you run to the store and pick him up a few teething rings and some *Orajel*? That's the only way we will get any sleep tonight."

"Yeah, I got it. Do you need anything else?" I walked up to her and wrapped my arm around her shoulder, then kissed her and Israel on their foreheads.

"No, just hurry back. I wanna put him to sleep so we can watch a movie."

"Are you sure Jay? Because I don't wanna have to go back out if you get one of your crazy cravings," I fussed at her as I walked towards the front door.

"You're the reason I'm like this so if you have to go back out when YOUR daughter craves something, so be it."

Yup, Janelle is pregnant. Unbeknownst to us, she probably got pregnant on our wedding night or soon thereafter. She went to the doctor for a regular checkup about a month and a half ago and the doctor told her that she was four months pregnant. That might be the other reason why she got some act right. She's now a little over six months along and we are having a baby girl.

These past few months have been crazy. After all is said and done, I love my son and I wouldn't give him up for anything. I hate that things went down the way that they did because hurting my wife was the absolute worst. I'm thankful that we made it through this rough patch and I'm looking forward to our future as a family, as dysfunctional as it may be.

THE END

Thank you for reading my first book. I hope you enjoyed and I really appreciate your support. If you could leave a review on Amazon, I would love to know what you think. Please like my Facebook page Kay Shanee's Reading Korner, follow me on Instagram @AuthorKayShanee, and check out my website at www.AuthorKayShanee.com for updates and news.

Made in United States
Orlando, FL
16 October 2024